SURVIVOR

A GRACED STORY

OTHER BOOKS BY AMANDA

Graced
Captive: A Graced Story
Bitten

The Graced Series

SURVIVOR

A Graced Story

AMANDA PILLAR

Published by Maatkare Books
www.amandapillar.com

Editor: Pete Kempshall

ISBN: 978-0-6480295-3-3

Cover Design: Ljiljana Romanovic © 2016
Internal Layout: Amanda Pillar © 2016

First Published February 2015

To the GMob. We shall endure

Prologue

Six months ago...

"What do you mean, 'Let the bitch go'?"

Billie wondered the same thing, her wheezing breath shooting pain throughout her chest. She thought she'd only been held by the asshole vampire and his crony for a few days – but the agony that coursed through her made it feel more like a few months. So Billie had no idea how long she'd really been stuck down here. They'd broken more of the bones in her body than she'd ever managed to before, and she was a Pinton City Guard. Getting beaten up was kind of part of the job description.

Pain radiated through her in waves. She was pretty sure the hip was broken, and that alone was enough to make her panic. How could she get away if she couldn't walk? Crawling was almost impossible, because they'd broken her left arm, too. She couldn't move without agony slicing through her, and it all but stopped her ability to think whenever the pain hit. But she was with it enough to remember that once a vampire kidnapped a human, they rarely let them go. She'd catalogued her fair share of corpses to know that without having to ponder it too much.

"We can't risk being caught with her." That was from the asshole vampire who'd plucked her off the street.

"Then just drain her dry and dump her in the Thyme." That was the crony.

She had no idea what either man looked like, but their speech patterns were distinct. Her kidnapper had a scratchy voice, like a human who'd spent most of his life drinking hard spirits and smoking a mountain of cigars. The crony had a smooth voice, cultured, like he was an aristo. He was at least educated; his vowels said as much. Not all vampires were aristos, but most went to wealthy schools.

Billie narrowed her eyes in the darkness at the second leech. Well, where she thought he was. She was being held in a pitch black room – probably a basement – but she could hear roughly where they were standing. The bastards. If only she could *move*, then she'd teach these fools a thing or two for abducting a city guard. But she couldn't. She'd probably pass out before she could get close enough to pinch them.

"She hasn't seen our faces, we could just let her go." The scratchy voice was almost wheedling.

"Why the fuck do you want to let her go?"

Billie winced. Hearing curse words in such an educated tone sounded strange to her. She was too used to the rough accents of the city guards.

It was a shame she hadn't seen what they looked like. Because if she did somehow manage to survive, she was going to come after them. And then she was going to break *their* bones. Sure, vampires healed super-fast, but they still felt pain. It just meant she could break them over and over again.

The sound of pacing feet reached her. "She's a bloody city guard!"

"You don't know that!"

"There are posters for her all over the city. She's been missing just a week and the guards are all over it."

There was a pause, and then the sound of flesh hitting flesh. Billie started to wonder if the crony was, in fact, the boss, and that the guy who'd snatched her was just the muscle.

"You idiot!"

"She wasn't in her uniform."

She'd been off duty – heading home after a night drinking at the local pub, the Severus Oracle. Odd name, but nice beer. Foolishly, she'd taken a shortcut through a small alley, where she'd been grabbed from behind. Her kidnapper had shoved a bag over her head, then knocked her out cold. Billie hadn't been unconscious for long, but she'd had a killer headache when she came to. And she'd been disorientated, carried over a shoulder, her stomach threatening revolt. When she'd finally worked out what was going on, she'd been dumped like a sack in a dark room.

Then the pain had started.

The crony/boss had stomped on her hip, shattering the bone, so she 'didn't get ideas about getting away'. And he'd snapped her arm, just to prove his point. It was then she'd known realistically that she wasn't likely to make it out of this alive. But hope was a powerful thing. And she'd always been a positive thinker.

They'd fed on her soon after breaking her arm, and she'd lost time through the drug-induced haze. It had felt like her whole body had come alive, tingles of pleasure zapping through her, to the point where she didn't feel the pain from her broken bones anymore. She didn't know how long it lasted, but she knew that she'd been defenseless the whole time. Billie had never allowed herself to become a vampire chew toy because she hadn't wanted to risk becoming bit-ridden – addicted to the high that came from vampire saliva. Now, it was the only thing she had to look forward to. The only time when the ache from her broken bones eased. And she hated herself for it. It had apparently only been seven days, and already she'd become weak.

What would the other guards think of her?

"So let's just get rid of her. When they find her body, they'll stop looking."

"If we drain her, then they'll know for sure it was a vampire."

"So?"

Billie swallowed. Her life really meant nothing to these leeches. At least the guards were looking for her. Someone would miss her when she was gone.

"They'll focus their murder investigation on vampires."

Which she guessed would only be a minor problem. Unless they had more kidnapped humans stashed away.

"We can't leave her alive, then they'll know for sure." That was from the boss. More pacing. "Slit her throat, and dump her. That way, the blood loss will be attributed to that. And no fresh bite marks."

Footsteps approached her then, and Billie tried to shift away, but she was helpless. Hands reached down and grabbed her, shoving a cloth bag that smelt of mold over her head. She screamed, but her head was slammed into the stone floor. Sunbursts of pain made her want to vomit.

"Make any more noise and we'll kill you."

"You're going to kill me anyway," Billie managed to mutter.

"Yes, but we could make it quick, or very long and painful. It's up to you."

Gee, Billie thought, *aren't they nice?* But she believed them.

The two of them picked her up, and she nearly passed out from the pain of her injuries. She bit back a loud moan, and thrashed against their holds. They hit her a couple more times, but the discomfort just bled into her existing agony.

She didn't know how much time had passed before they pulled the sack off her head. The smell of the Thyme River reached her – piss, trash and fish –

and she could hear the water moving; a gentle lapping against the retaining walls built to prevent flooding. She couldn't see much, which meant that it was the middle of the night.

A shadow loomed over her, the strange scent of cucumber and rose wafting toward her. Maybe her sense of smell was working harder, she thought, because she was all but blind. If she lived, she'd make sure she never forgot that cologne.

"Just do it." That was from the boss.

And then her hair was grabbed and her head jerked back. A cold knife pressed to her throat.

"Say goodbye, bitch."

The sharp burn of the knife as it cut into her made her breath seize. And then she was pitching forward, into the Thyme. A scream burst from her lips as her body splashed into the cold water, and then the river closed over her head.

CHAPTER ONE

Current day

"Billie!"

Blinking, Billie stared at the paperwork spread out before her on the metal desk. One yellowy page held a list of current investigations, with the other sheets surrounding it containing their progress reports.

She looked up and gave a half-smile at the huge man in front of her. "Yes?"

"You all right?" Mikael Smythe was the Pinton City Guard's Night Captain. He propped his hip against the corner of her desk. He was so tall she had to crane her neck to look up at him, and his skin was a beautiful black that absorbed light. She was envious of the hue; hers was a caramel color that showed every scar.

And boy, did she have a few.

Then again, it probably didn't matter what color her skin was. She'd never be able to hide the nasty big line across her throat. How she'd survived her river dive was pure luck. A trash collector had been on a barge that night, and had heard her splash and scream. Rather than ignoring it, as was the norm, he'd gone to investigate, and spotted her bobbing in the water. She didn't remember any of it, just waking up in a hospital, her neck swathed in bandages and her limbs immobilized due to the breaks. She'd gone back to work as soon as she could – but that had been months after she'd been dragged out of the Thyme.

Months where she hadn't been able to search for her attackers. Even now, she had a list tucked away in her drawer of possible leads and avenues for investigation. But her case was a cold one, and she had other priorities. Plus, with the number of dead humans found every week in Pinton, it made it hard to work out where to start.

But that didn't mean she'd stopped looking over her shoulder. She knew the vampires would come for her one day, she just had no idea when. Well, they'd come for her, if they bothered to check whether she survived or not. She wasn't taking the chance they were lazy.

"I'm doing great," Billie lied belatedly.

Mikael's dark brown gaze said he didn't believe her, but he didn't call her on her bullshit. That's what she liked about the guard captain. He was fair, honest, but also understanding. It wasn't to say that you should risk pissing him off, because that was always a dangerous move. But as long as you lied for a good reason, he'd let it slide.

He'd let a lot of her lies slide.

"I hate to ask this of you, but I need a letter to be dropped off to an aristo household." Mikael's deep voice rumbled through the room, the high ceilings almost causing it to echo. They were behind the main reception of the guard house, in the open plan office area, and the dozen or so metal desks surrounding hers were vacant. As Mikael's assistant, her desk was in the row behind his, which was neat as a pin. There were only a few full-time office staff like her, and the rest had a rotating system, for when they came in to file their reports. Their desks were all tidy as well. Mikael didn't tolerate disorder.

Except for hers.

Then Mikael's words sank in. Her new black and brown outfit suddenly felt like it was choking her. She fiddled with the black scarf around her neck, her personal addition to the mandatory uniform. Billie didn't know what she was going to do when the weather grew warmer. "A letter dropped to an aristo?"

She'd obviously failed at trying to play it cool when Mikael's face turned sympathetic. Almost pitying, but not quite. She didn't think she could have handled that. "I'd ask someone else, but everyone is out. And I have to head home to look after my son."

Mikael had a boy who was about ten years old. From the snippets he'd mentioned, Billie gathered that the kid was having a rough time at school. He was 'too sensitive' according to the Night Captain and his teachers, but Mikael seemed at a loss as to how to change that without traumatizing the lad. And Billie knew all about trauma.

"No, no, it's okay." Billie forced her voice into sounding positive. Hopefully it would be a human aristo. That would be fine. And the likelihood of her bumping into the actual aristo who lived at the estate would be slim to none. After all, rich people didn't tend to answer their own doors.

He winced a little. "I really am sorry, I wouldn't ask otherwise."

"Really, I can do it." Not that she wanted to, but she didn't want to be treated differently because of her…past. Although, her 'past' was the reason she was now stuck with desk work, rather than bashing skulls like she used to. Even though she'd survived, she hadn't come out of her ordeal whole. Billie wouldn't risk her partner's life on her not being able to step in on a fight, or because she froze in panic.

Mikael strode over to his desk and retrieved the letter. When he handed it to her, she looked down at the thick creamy parchment sealed with the black wax of the City Guard. It must be official. They didn't normally bother with that level of sophistication.

"Should I know what's in here?" Billie said. "In case they ask."

Mikael sighed. "We sent out a letter to all the aristo families to let them know that Choosing someone is forbidden until King Johan says otherwise."

Transforming someone into a vampire is now illegal? *What happened?*

"Why is the City Guard delivering these messages?" She would have thought that the king's staff would have done that. If it was a royal decree.

Mikael shrugged. "We're meant to enforce it. I don't know how we will, but that's what the king says. The stupid Palace Guard won't do anything about it, that's for sure."

The Palace Guard was comprised of vampires, whereas the City Guard was humans. The City Guard had jurisdiction right up to the palace gates, where the Palace Guard took over. They rarely ventured into the city.

Billie held up the letter. "But what about this one?"

"It was missed." Mikael looked a little embarrassed. "I was reminded of this fact in a meeting with the King's Council. So it needs to get done tonight."

Well, this morning technically. It was nearing six am and the sun was coming up. But she wasn't about to quibble. It meant she got to leave work early, and the sun would be in the sky. While vampires liked to keep night hours, they did venture out during the day. It just meant there were fewer of them, and it made it harder for them to participate in clandestine activities.

Running her fingers over the letter, Billie leaned down awkwardly and grabbed her satchel off the floor. It was brown leather, and worn on the sides. But she loved it. Her foster mother had given it to her when she became a guard. Slinging the pack over her shoulder, Billie grasped her metal cane from where she'd leaned it against the desk. She didn't always need it, but the colder weather made her hip ache. It had never healed properly, since it had started to set while she was being held by the vampires. But at least she was alive and could walk.

"I'll drop it off and head home, if that's okay?"

Mikael nodded, and then plucked his jacket from

the back of his chair. "Sure, Kyle is due back in soon to finish his shift."

City guards tended to work in groups of four, and Billie had been teamed with a guy called Oliver Brindle. The other half of their group had been Kyle McInnes and Elle Brown. But Billie had been taken off active duty the moment she was found in hospital, and recently, Elle had gone missing. Even though they'd had a funeral for her, rumor had it that she was actually alive. Billie might be the captain's assistant, but she wasn't privy to that kind of information, even if it were true.

"I'll be sorry to miss Kyle," Billie said. They didn't tend to see each other all that much, as Kyle avoided spending time doing paperwork, and that's all she did nowadays. But at least he and Oliver made a good team.

"Hah. Don't tell him that. His ego is big enough as it is."

Billie chuckled, not that she really felt like it. But she knew how to act normal. As she began limping toward the doorway, the polished stone floor reflecting her broken visage back at her, she felt Mikael's eyes on her. She knew that it ate him up – him and every other guard she bumped into – that they hadn't found her in time. That the only reason she was still with them was sheer bloody luck. But she couldn't let them think she needed protecting, otherwise they'd never let her leave the building.

And her work was all she had left.

CHAPTER THREE

Sometimes, being a spy sucked.

It wasn't all ballrooms, romance, and extravagant feats of duplicity, as the racy novels by Whitmoreson would have you believe. No, it involved a lot of watching, waiting and *patience*. The latter of which was supposedly a virtue. Vere didn't tend to agree with that assertion.

Plus, if Vere had to pretend to drink any more of the insipid ale that had been sitting in front of him, he was sure he'd go mad. He was so close to returning home that he could almost taste the fine whiskey from his spirits collection. But so far, his contact had been a no-show.

The packet of papers in Vere's pocket reminded him he had one more task to do before he could climb the stairs to his house, enjoy a hot bath and have a decent night's sleep. The king needed copies of his latest field notes. They were written in a code that was only known to King Johan and his most trusted spies. Anyone who managed to get their hands on his reports would think Vere was the most boring letter writer in Pinton.

At least now he had a real reason for visiting the Crystal Palace, and he didn't have to try and sneak in. A few years ago, he'd been caught by the Palace Guard, and that had been…awkward. For all intents and purposes, Vere was 'friend' of the king. His father, Baron Moore, and his brother, the Honorable Dickwad – well, that wasn't really his title, but Vere had never really been one for ceremony when it came to family – found it incredible the king *liked* him. They suspected it was because Vere offered their monarch *personal favors*, but Vere didn't particularly care what they thought. The less they pondered his reasons for being with the king, the better.

Vere glanced up from his musings, eyeing the room for his contact. He'd only met the other man twice before. The fellow was a suspicious sort, who dealt in information about Pinton's cits. Rumor had it that there'd been a lot of unrest lately; that one of the wealthiest marketers of human flesh had been removed from the game. Vere had received a note from the king demanding he look into it on his return from Skarva. So Vere booked the meeting in, despite having only just returned to the city after a year's absence.

But while his contact had responded saying to meet him at the Tipsy Lantern at four in the afternoon, that time had come and gone. The bar's patrons were all human, and nobody paid him any attention. It wasn't the kind of establishment that drew vampire clientele, or were, for that matter. Not that there were many weres in Pinton, Vere admitted. Scanning the crowd, he took in the mix of dock workers and tradesmen. Vere's travelling clothes of wool and calico blended right in.

The doors banged open, and a man shuffled into the tavern. His eyes darted over the drinkers, skipping by the barmaids. Finally. Vere's man had arrived. He held up his tankard in acknowledgment, when the fellow's eyes reached him. His contact moved through the crowd, heading straight for the smoky corner.

The man nodded at Vere, then pulled out a chair and sat. His face was drawn and tired, like he'd been put through the wringer. "Joe."

"Jim."

Vere's name was as much Joe as Kevin's was Jim, but Vere let the other man believe his identity was secure. Kevin's surname, however, was Smitherson, and he worked as a bodyguard to Olive Brown. Olive ostensibly ran an agency that supplied human servants to aristos, but she also had a steady and profitable side-business in selling slaves. Kevin only peddled Vere information that didn't compromise his boss' business, and that was fine with him. Any information was worthwhile.

Vere held up his ale and pretended to take a sip. "You appear tired. Bad week?"

Kevin looked at him. "More like a bad month. You haven't heard?"

"Heard?" Vere didn't like being at a disadvantage.

"My boss, Olive, was killed. As was my brother, Bjorn."

Vere set his tankard back on the scarred table. "I'm sorry to hear that." This very well might be the last meeting he had with Kevin, then.

Kevin hung his head for a moment. "She was my great-aunt." Then he shrugged. "But, she was a horrendous bitch. So no great loss."

People were messed up. "I'm sorry for your brother, then."

"Thanks. He was an idiot. But I loved him."

"That explains the rumors I heard," Vere said.

"Rumors?"

"That there'd been some shady business going on with some powerful cits."

"I don't know where you get your intel from, but it's right as usual. I can't add much more, though."

Vere slid across a bag of coins. Kevin picked it up, checking the weight. Then he narrowed his eyes. "Before Olive died, she had some interesting information for me, Joe."

"Really?" Vere drummed his fingers against his tankard.

Joe looked at him. "Turns out, you aren't the simple human merchant you'd have me believe."

Vere widened his pale-colored eyes. "We are never as simple as we'd like to think. Or state."

"No, but then I never pretended I was human."

Vere straightened in his chair.

"Olive made it her business to know all about the aristo families in Pinton. Turns out – to my surprise – that the man I was selling information to was none other than the second son of Baron Moore."

Fuck.

Part of the reason Vere was a spy – and one favored by his monarch – was because he could pass as a human or vampire. At least to humans. If he'd blown his cover…

Vere smiled, showing his teeth, but no fang. "Come now, vampires have purple eyes."

"Yes, they do. And I just took you for having gray eyes, like me. But then, you don't seem to be like me at all." Kevin peered at him closely. "No, you just have really, really pale lavender-colored eyes."

Vered sighed. "I never said I was human."

"No, but you implied it. And not just to me. To your other contacts in the city, as well."

Vere hid his surprise. Olive had more connections than even he'd believed. It was a good thing the bloody woman was dead.

Kevin clearly wasn't stating his newfound knowledge without a reason. "What will your silence on this matter cost?"

"A lot more than this measly bag of coin. I need to get out of town. Give me a horse, coin, and a letter of passage out the kingdom, and none of your other contacts will ever hear from me again."

It was a costly bargain. Vere could just kill the man and be done with it, but from the look in Kevin's steely eyes, it wouldn't be quite as easy as he'd once thought.

"Done."

Chapter Four

Billie told herself to just take three deep breaths.

In. Out.

In. Out.

In. Out.

There.

She could do this. She could. It was just a set of stairs. Ten of them. Made from bluestone. Easy. She walked up stairs like that all the time, even though it hurt her. So what, that the entry was actually a set of double doors, with a rather forbidding-looking knocker made from bronze? So what, that the twin pots of standard roses set either side of the doorway were extravagantly in bloom, their crimson petals an unfortunate reminder of blood? And so what, that the house was so tall she had to tilt her neck back to see the roof?

So what?

A servant would answer the door, she'd drop the letter off and the job would be complete. Billie could happily report to Mikael that she had no issues handing the piece of parchment over.

She just had to get to the door.

Her breath fogged in the morning air as she stood staring at the estate's entrance from the sidewalk. The scarf she had around her neck wasn't big enough to wrap around her lower face to warm her poor nose. Mornings were surprisingly cold this time of year. She probably looked a bit like a thug, with her black scarf, big black jacket and black pants. But she couldn't help that. *Just do it*, her mind snapped. *You look like a fool.*

And she probably did. Sighing to herself, she took another deep breath and then stepped forward. Her hope that this was a human aristo estate had died on her walk over from the City Guard building. Why would she be sending a letter about Choosing someone to a human family? Sure, humans liked to get Chosen – longevity was a hook to most people – but the guards couldn't really enforce the ban like vampires could. Guards couldn't, after all, just *not* Choose people.

Billie shuffled closer to the stairs. Looking to her left and right, she saw that the sidewalk was mostly empty, although there was a man in a greatcoat approaching from the east. Squinting, she couldn't tell if he was a vampire or human from this distance.

You're stalling again.

Huffing, she placed her walking stick on the first stair, and used it to help drag her right leg up, then followed it with her left. She'd gone three steps when she felt someone staring at her.

Billie half-turned to see the man in the greatcoat

watching her from the base of the stairs. Shiny brown hair escaped the hood of his coat, and few strands had caught on his dark red lips. She didn't care about his pretty face though, her gaze was locked on his eyes. They were so pale, she couldn't tell if they were gray or purple.

Human or vampire?

Neither of them moved for a few seconds, then the stranger strode up the stairs to stand next to her. She wasn't short, at five feet ten, but he loomed over her, six feet four, she guessed, and solidly muscled. The coat didn't hide that. But vampires didn't need to be muscled to be strong enough to overpower her.

"Can I help you?" His voice was low and warm, and it made her frown. He smiled then, as if reassuringly. His accent said he was educated at a wealthy school, which meant he was either an aristo, or someone striving to be one.

"I'm just delivering something to the household." Billie didn't bother smiling back, she just held up the sealed letter.

His eyes alighted on the black wax, and his expression grew serious. "I can take it inside."

While Billie would have dearly loved to have the duty taken from her, people didn't just show up on random streets and do favors for city guards. "How do I even know you live here?"

He spread his hands out in a non-threatening gesture. "Why would I lie?"

Billie wanted to fold her arms across her chest, but she couldn't let go of her cane. It was metal, so she could probably whack him with it if he got difficult.

"You tell me."

"Tough. I like that."

Billie narrowed her eyes. "I'll just take the letter up now."

Facing forward, she lifted the cane and then repeated her whole bloody useless stair-climbing procedure. To think, before she'd been attacked, she hadn't ever thought twice about climbing stairs – not unless there were hundreds of the stupid things. She hadn't ever thought about how hard it was for people who didn't have use of both their legs to get around. And now it made her feel really shallow. She'd taken being able-bodied for granted. So she'd made it a goal to help people like her obtain work at places like the City Guard. The others supported her, but she wasn't sure if it was driven from pity or not. And while it chafed, she wasn't going to care. If it got her – and others like her – what they needed, then so be it.

The man followed her slow progress. "I really do live here, I can take the letter."

"It's fine." Her voice came out rough, since she was clenching her teeth.

Finally, the top. Sighing in relief, Billie slammed the fancy knocker down. The door opened, and she was so peeved at the man for offering her help, she just thrust the note at the butler, never shifting her glare from the stranger standing next to her.

"Sir," the butler said from behind her.

The man nodded at the servant, but he didn't go inside. "Please take the letter to Father. I'll let myself in later."

Then the door closed, and she was left outside

with him, the roses standing guard on either side. Billie sensed he was waiting for her to say something, but if he wanted an apology, he had another thing coming. "So you live here. Good for you."

Straightening her spine, she then started the equally slow process of descending. He kept up with her, and didn't say anything while she maneuvered herself awkwardly down the stairs. Reaching the bottom, she planted her cane on the ground and turned to leave.

A hand gently took hold of her upper arm. Looking over her shoulder at her, the stranger's pale eyes seemed to stare at her in concern. She shuddered slightly. Billie had been avoiding contact with vampires ever since she'd been dragged from the river. She knew it wasn't rational, that most vampires didn't kidnap humans. They had slaves – and blood dens – for their food source. But she couldn't silence that part of her brain that screamed they were all predators.

And she was prey.

His voice reached her. "Where do you live?"

Billie blinked, frowning down at his hand. Vampire or not, she wasn't about to tell a stranger on the street her address. "None of your business."

He let go. "I just want to walk you home."

"That's nice." She turned away.

"You know where I live."

Billie snorted, she couldn't help it. Then a realization struck her. "Are you going to just follow me anyway?"

He strode into her line of vision and gave her a

half-smile. "Probably."

Billie sighed. She hadn't figured that she'd find herself a shadow. Helpful people weren't all that common in her experience. It made her suspicious. "Fine. You can walk me most of the way there. But not to the door. I don't want some strange psycho knowing where I live."

He placed a hand over his heart. "You wound me."

Rolling her eyes, Billie walked toward the Pittbrough Street intersection. She could see dark carriages, bright multi-colored hackneys, and gaudily dressed hawkers at the junction. It was the main road through the city, so it should be safe enough for her to walk alone – or with a stranger. She'd learned her lesson; no more back alleys.

The aristo kept pace with her, remaining strangely silent. After all but bullying her into accepting his help, she was surprised he'd managed to keep his own counsel this long. She half-turned her head in his direction. He was staring straight ahead, a slight smile dancing across his mouth. It was such a shame that his mouth was so kissable.

The thought almost pulled her up short. She hadn't thought about kissing anyone in the last six months.

"What?" He turned to look at her.

Billie managed to blurt, "What's your name?"

His smile grew, but it wasn't toothy like a vampire's grin. "Vere."

She snorted, not sure she believed him. "'Vere' what?"

"What's *your* name?"

"I asked first."

"Vere Radcliffe."

It didn't mean anything to her, but somehow it made her feel more empowered. Now that she knew his name, he wasn't a stranger. Well, not entirely.

They reached the corner of Pittbrough Street, and Billie inhaled the smell of something spicy and delicious. Looking to the left, she spotted a small stall, its gaudy orange and yellow fabric roof fluttering in the morning breeze. A pot of stew was simmering on a bed of hot coals, with warm crunchy bread in a basket on the counter for buyers. She had a couple of coins in her pocket, and was tempted to buy some for her dinner, but the stranger made her hesitate.

What would he care what she ate?

But he was an aristo, and she doubted he'd ever eaten something as mediocre as street food. As she dithered, a stream of hackneys and carriages trundled by, returning revelers to their homes, or taking those wealthier than her to their morning shifts.

"Now it's your turn."

Billie paused. "My turn for what?"

"To tell me your name."

"Oh, right."

"Your name is 'oh, right'?"

Billie glared at him. So he was a smartass? An aristo smartass?

Thumping her cane against the sidewalk, Billie began walking down Pittbrough Street toward Light Street. It was the quickest way home, and also one of the busiest. Dodging around slow-moving aristo leeches – always careful to keep a safe distance – she made her way across the busy street. She felt, rather than heard, Vere following her.

"My name is Billie," she said.

"Billie." The way he said it made her stop and stare at him.

Suddenly, she was half-picked up and dragged to the other side of the road. Then Vere's face was leaning down toward her. He was frowning. "Don't just stop in the middle of the road!"

"I–"

"You what?"

Billie tucked her chin into the folds of her scarf. "I wasn't thinking."

"Clearly," he muttered.

"What's it to you, anyway?" Billie asked.

Chapter Five

What was it to him?

It was a valid question, and one Vere should be asking himself. Why did he care that the city guard had nearly gotten herself run over on the busiest street in Pinton? She was just a human, and one he probably would have never met if not for her knocking on the door to his father's townhouse. But he found he hadn't liked the idea of her putting herself in danger.

They were standing in front of the Rutherford Hotel. Billie didn't seem like the type of person to have entered the august establishment – she fidgeted just looking at the hotel past his shoulder. It was ornate, with a color scheme of creams, blues and golds. He'd visited it once or twice on former liaisons.

"You getting yourself killed in front of me will be a pain in the ass." He folded his arms across his chest, but inwardly he groaned. Way to make himself sound like a complete dickhead.

Those dark brown eyes narrowed at him

menacingly. She was of average height, and pretty, but not stunning. Not like vampires or weres would be. But then, they were like that to attract prey. Her firm chin suggested that she was stubborn, and he liked her strength of will. Walking up those stairs, refusing the easy way out? Being skeptical of a stranger and relying on herself and her abilities? Vere had to say, he found that horribly attractive.

And then there were her lips; full and soft, and they'd been the first thing he'd noticed about her. Which was a bad thing. Because when he saw her lips it made him want to kiss her, and that was just a really terrible idea. She was a human, and she worked for the City Guard. They were a combination that didn't go well with an aristo vampire. Especially not one perceived to be a socialite who happened to be a spy on the side.

And wasn't he jumping to crazy conclusions awfully fast?

She didn't rise to his bait, though. "The way home is pretty safe, I don't need a bodyguard."

"Humor me."

"Why should I?"

"Because."

She mumbled something he didn't quite catch, but she started walking toward Light Street. There was a nice restaurant on the corner, which specialized in chocolates and coffees. It was expensive, so he doubted she'd ever had the chance to venture inside. Suddenly, he wanted to take her there.

"Did you want to get a coffee?" he asked.

Billie froze, then turned slowly around. Her gaze

wandered up and down his frame, and he hoped she liked what she saw. *Idiot.* He was helping her home simply because she couldn't defend herself properly. And he didn't like anyone being defenseless. After having grown up with his father and brother, he knew what happened to slaves and those with less power.

No one deserved that.

It's why they didn't own slaves anymore. Technically, a slave owner could do whatever they wanted to their 'stock' – but when every slave who enters your household dies within a few months? Even the king hears about that kind of thing. And if the king 'suggests' that slave owning is obviously not appropriate for Baron Moore, then Baron Moore doesn't own any more slaves. At least, not publicly.

The Baron could still have human servants, but their death-rate was closely watched. Anything that seemed suspicious, the Palace Guard would be on their doorstep, ready to investigate. Plus, if something happened to a servant, his father would have to pay a death-tax. And his father was frugal with his coin.

"A coffee?"

Part of him wanted to take the offer back, but he didn't. He might be starting something here that could only end badly. But then, nothing at all might happen. He met her no-nonsense gaze, her brown eyes huge in her face. "A coffee."

They'd reached the corner of Light and Pittbrough streets. The specialty store, Luscious, was right behind them, its large windows displaying a variety of chocolates he could barely name. While he relied on blood to sustain himself, he could eat and he did. But he'd gathered that chocolate was more of a female obsession. There were always exceptions to that rule, though. Maybe Billie was one. Personally, he liked coffee.

Billie raised one dark eyebrow at him. "In here?"

The strong smell of chocolate permeated the air, and he saw a spark of excitement ignite in her serious eyes. He shrugged, even though that had been his intention all along. "Sure."

She thumped her metal cane on the ground. Not for the first time, he wondered why she needed it. Had she been born with a physical issue? Or was it an injury? She wore a city guard's uniform, so it could easily be the latter.

But her ability to push through her discomfort and live her life, and work her kind of job?

Freaking impressive.

"You're paying?"

He grinned then, his careful-I'm-not-showing-any-fangs smile. "Sure."

CHAPTER SIX

It was strange to find herself sitting at a tiny corner table in one of the most exclusive restaurants in Pinton. And with an aristo she'd only just met. But Billie wasn't silly enough to let an opportunity like this to go to waste. Sure, she might be using him, but she wasn't quite sure what he wanted in return. At least she knew he wasn't doing this just to sleep with her. Most men found her cane and disability a bit hard to deal with. Like she was at risk of breaking. Or worse, that she'd cling to them and expect them to help her in this new life.

She was probably being a little uncharitable.

But the couple of times she'd tried to ask a guy out – mostly just as friends – the refusal had been swift and painful. Not to her heart, though; that organ hadn't been engaged for a long time. Even before she'd been taken.

Looking around the restaurant, she took in the dim lighting, and the wonderful booths that lined one wall. Gilded picture frames hung above the maroon-leather seats, highlighting lovely paintings of flower-filled fields, chocolate delights and aristos of bygone times. Closer to their table, there was a counter filled with all kinds of chocolates; from sugar-coated extravagances, to glistening truffles. The smell of melted chocolate made her mouth water.

Where she and Vere sat, there was a small cluster of round tables, varying with two and four metal chairs each. Theirs was decorated with a small glass cup with a lit candle inside, cutlery, linen napkins and a menu they had to share. Reaching forward, she plucked the menu from its place in the center of the table and read over its contents. Her eyes bugged a little at the prices, but she decided she didn't feel bad about making him pay. He was an aristo who was following her home. She was a city guard.

Vere leaned forward, resting his elbows on the small table. "Do you know what you want?"

Billie gave a short laugh. "Everything."

A slightly panicked look crossed his features. "Really?"

She took pity on him. Maybe his allowance wasn't that great. She figured he must be a younger son. "Yes, but I'll get sick if I order too much."

Handing the menu over to him, she kept a straight face as he gave it a cursory glance then set it down.

"Know what you want already?"

"I'm not really a chocolate fan."

Billie shut her eyes, waving a hand in the air. "You are dead to me."

A strange rumble-laugh sound emerged from him. Most undignified, she thought, for an aristo. She was coming to realize though, that he wasn't like what she'd expected from the upper class. He seemed more relaxed…more human.

"I like coffee." He gave an odd one-shouldered shrug.

"Coffee," she scoffed. It wasn't bad, and she sure needed it in the morning, but coffee over chocolate? Not in this lifetime. "More chocolate for me then."

"Didn't you just say that you'd get sick if you ate too much?"

Billie allowed herself a smile. "Didn't anyone ever tell you that a man shouldn't get between a woman and her chocolate?"

"No." He smiled back at her, and gee, that was an experience she could have lived without. It sent him from handsome to devastating. "But I'll take that advice on board now."

The waiter arrived, dressed in a pressed white shirt, with a starched high collar, and black pants. His outfit would have cost three times as much as her city guard uniform. She hoped the shop paid for it. Billie ordered a chocolate pudding and a hot chocolate. She was thankful Vere kept his opinion to himself on her choices, and ordered a black coffee.

Once the waiter had left, he said, "Aren't you going to take your scarf off? It's warm in here."

Billie's enjoyment died. "It's okay. I like wearing it."

Vere frowned. He looked down at her cane, then back up at her scarf. "You're sweating. You should take it off."

She could feel the slight sheen of perspiration on

her skin above the scarf. But she didn't want to take it off. In the guard house, people couldn't seem to stop looking at the scar, and she didn't want to be a freak show.

"It's fine."

Vere narrowed his eyes. "You said the same thing in the same tone when you were struggling up those bloody stairs." He tapped a finger against the tabletop. "So what are you hiding under the scarf?"

"Who says I'm hiding anything?"

He stared at her.

She sighed. If he wanted to see so badly, then sure. Why not? As she unwound the black material from around her neck, his eyes locked on her throat. She draped the scarf over the back of her chair. Turning to face him, she tried not to think about the purple-pink scar that marred her caramel skin.

Vere's expression went utterly blank. His eyes dipped down to her cane, then back to her neck. "You survived having your throat slit?" He met her gaze, seeming slightly...awestruck.

"Clearly." She touched a finger to the edge of the scar.

"Did you catch whoever did it? It was someone you were trying to apprehend?" His voice was low and intense.

The waiter returned then, placing her hot chocolate and his coffee on the table. "Your pudding is on the way." His pretentious air made Billie's teeth clench, but she smiled anyway. Then his eyes dipped to her scar.

Vere's voice cut in. "Thank you. Leave us."

The waiter disappeared.

She wanted to put her scarf back on. But wearing it would be another victory for her attackers. "No. I know it was two vampires, and they grabbed me when I was off duty. They slit my throat and dumped me in the Thyme to avoid getting caught."

She shrugged and picked up her drink, appearing nonchalant. "Unlucky for them, I survived."

CHAPTER SEVEN

Should he tell her?

But if she had a problem with vampires, then she'd leave, and she'd only just taken a sip of her drink. Her eyes had actually shut as she savored the taste. He couldn't ruin her moment, any more than he already had, at any rate.

Was it sad that if he had a romantic bone in his body, he'd have fallen a little bit in love with her? Mental strength was a trait he admired above all else. And for her to survive what had happened to her, not only sane, but with a dry sense of humor? It was a killer combination, no pun intended. Humor, after all, was second on his list of 'traits I like'.

"How long ago was it?" It was hard to tell from her scar. A vampire would recover from something like that in a day, but humans took longer to mend. Hopefully he didn't give himself away with the question.

She put her cup down. A smidgen of chocolate was on the corner of her mouth, but he didn't say anything. Mostly because he was worried he'd offer to wipe it himself. Or lick it. "You didn't hear about it?"

"I've been out of town for a year," he admitted.

"Oh." She looked down at her cup, and closed both palms around it. "Six months ago."

"And you're back at work?" He kept the incredulity from his voice.

"Yeah, so?" She seemed defensive, her lips pressed together in a thin line.

"It's very admirable," he admitted.

Her eyes widened. Then she looked down at her chocolate. The waiter appeared and placed the pudding in front of her. He also left two spoons, as if they were going to share her treat. Vere said nothing, just watched the human work. He could see how the waiter responded to Billie with a slight air of contempt, like she didn't deserve to be in a place like this. As far as Vere was concerned, she should be anywhere she wanted.

When the waiter left, Billie took a spoonful of chocolate pudding. She actually groaned when it reached her mouth. The lemon scent of her intensified with her delight. Suddenly, it became uncomfortable to sit there with her. That sound…it went straight to his groin.

Bad Vere.

"I take it that's good?" he asked with a slight smile, hiding his awkwardness.

Billie looked up, a blush on her cheeks. "Yeah. Do you want some?" She held out the second spoon reluctantly.

"It's all yours," he said.

CHAPTER EIGHT

Billie couldn't believe that she'd actually gone out on a date. With someone she just met, who was a protective pain in the butt. She wasn't sure why he'd decided that she needed an escort home, but their stop for chocolate had ended up being enjoyable, and not just because of the food.

They were standing on the corner of Court Road and Rock Street. It was less busy here, and there were no lamps to illuminate the area. But the sun had well and truly risen now, and the cobbled road and bluestone buildings were bathed in a soft morning glow.

"I live near here. I don't care that you bought me horribly expensive chocolate, I'm not letting you know my address." Billie smiled, but she meant what she said.

He gave an exaggerated sigh, then looked up and down the street. "I guess it's safe enough."

"It was always safe."

"No, it wasn't." His gaze locked on her scarf, tied

back around her throat, and then dropped to her cane.

"I was in a side alley when that happened. Only main roads for me now."

Nodding, he stepped closer to her, and she swore she could feel his body heat emanating across the small distance. His voice was low, almost gravelly. "But things still happen in broad daylight."

And he kissed her.

Just softly, a lingering press of his mouth to hers, his tongue darting out to tease the seam of her lips. He tasted like coffee, and she thought she might like that drink a whole lot more than she had this morning.

The kiss was over quickly though, and he turned and headed back the way they came. He held his hand up once in a salute, then turned the corner and disappeared from view. But she was rooted to the spot, her fingers pressed to her lips.

CHAPTER NINE

A week later

Billie was back at her desk at work, sorting through reports. It seemed like her life consisted of filing one piece of paper after another. But it was work, and it gave her purpose. And it stopped her from thinking about a certain aristo with very soft lips. And a slightly wicked tongue.

"Hey, Billie?"

Dr. Alice Reive was standing in front of her desk. The coroner's curly auburn hair was tied back in a bun, and her short curvy figure was neatly dressed in her uniform red shirt and black pants. She was holding a clipboard. That couldn't be a good sign.

Then again, the fact that Alice had left the basement morgue probably wasn't a good sign in and of itself. The dead-person doctor rarely spent time in the upstairs offices. And Billie didn't venture down to the morgue often herself. Not because dead people bothered her – she'd seen her fair share of corpses – but there were at least two flights of stairs to contend with.

"Hey Alice, what brings you up here?" Billie gave her a smile. She liked the coroner, even though she spent all her time with cadavers. Alice was smart, kind, and most of all, understood Billie's dark sense of humor.

"I just had a body brought in that I thought you might find of interest." Alice placed the clipboard on Billie's desk, then grabbed a nearby chair and brought it over. Those chairs were heavy. Alice was stronger than her short frame gave her credit for. Billie picked up the report. Tingles of alarm spread through her.

D.o.D: Fifth Day, Third Month

Time & Location of autopsy: 20:00, City Morgue, Pinton

Species: Human

Sex: Female

Height: Five feet two inches

Weight: 100 pounds

Age: 20-30

Eye color: Brown

Hair color: Brown

Skin color: Brown

Cause of death: Exsanguination

Trauma: The victim suffered a fractured pelvis – the right pelvis (ilium) was shattered from vertical force. Left arm transversely fractured. Multiple bite marks indicate the victim was fed on by vampires for a number of weeks before she died. The ilium and humerus had begun healing,

also indicating a time in captivity.
    General notes: Body was discovered in the Thyme.

Billie's heart was thundering, blood pounding in her ears. This poor girl had been abducted by the same kidnappers who had taken her. It had to be. Everything about the crimes matched – except the time in captivity. Although, Billie hadn't seen a missing person's case come in with this girl's description, she was sure of it. She'd kept her eyes peeled for any crimes that might show similarities to hers, and she'd been slowly working through the last six months of backlog, in her free time.

"Billie?"

She met Alice's concerned stare. "Sorry, but this…"

Alice nodded, her expression somber. "I brought this to you because I read your file."

"You read my file?" A stone lodged itself somewhere in her stomach.

A little ashamed, Alice nodded. "I *am* a doctor, even though I work mostly with cadavers. I wanted to see if there was something I could do to help your recovery. But your pelvis had already started to heal, and your arm had already been re-broken and set…"

Alice had tried to help her? She couldn't be annoyed at the intrusion on her privacy, even though part of her wanted to be.

"So when the body came in, and I catalogued her wounds…I just knew you had to see this."

"Thank you for bringing it to my attention." She handed the file back. Billie wanted to keep it, to pore over it, but that wasn't her place. "Can I get a copy?"

"Sure…Kyle didn't want me to show you – he brought the body in – but if it was me, I'd want to know." Something dark burned in Alice's eyes, and Billie had the revelation that Alice might have been wounded by someone in her past. She wondered if they'd ever been caught and punished. She hoped they had.

Billie gave a pathetic attempt at a smile. "Thanks for ignoring him."

Alice's expression lightened. "Any time."

Billie drummed her fingers on the desk, thinking. If this had happened to her, and at least one other girl...

"Alice, can you please check if you have any other files that match the latest girl's?"

The coroner looked thoughtful. "How far back should I search?"

"The attackers are vampires. They live a long time. As far back as you can."

She nodded. "Done. It might take a while, though."

"As long as it takes," Billie said. She'd been searching through any and all murders in Pinton over the last six months, however, if she could narrow her search down to specific injuries... It might help catch the assholes who almost killed her, and who did murder an innocent young woman.

Alice turned on her heel to leave, then looked back. "I hope you find the bastards, and make them pay."

Billie's fingers curled around the handle of her

cane. "Thank you."

CHAPTER TEN

Vere had been summoned to the Crystal Palace. It had been a little over a week since he'd returned, and he'd been grateful for the appointment. Living with his brother and father was a special kind of torture he could really do without. If he knew he'd be staying for any appreciable amount of time in Pinton, he'd get his own place. But he didn't know where the king might send him next.

It wasn't that his father abused him, or even really spoke to him. But he'd made it more than clear when Vere was a child that he was considered to be nothing more than property. His mother – her identity still a secret – had contested the breeding contract she'd signed with the Baron: Vere's father hadn't told her that he'd also impregnated another woman, mere months before. His mother had been led to believe that Vere would be the heir, not the spare, and so had challenged the legal agreement. But she'd lost, and the case – and her identity – had been locked away by the court.

Vere had learned all this when he was five, when his brother Bryce had been visited by *his* mother. The truth had been laid bare by the Baron, who preferred her to be an absent parent, so her influence would not affect his all-important first son. Bryce's mother had never returned. But before she'd left, she'd delivered a scathing lecture on Bryce's attitude, though Baron Moore had *not* been pleased by her assessment. Bryce could do no wrong. She was classed as a moron of the highest order.

Baron Moore still considered her wrong when Bryce had grown into a teen and had developed a passion for blood and violence. When it became clear he could not – and had no desire to – control his activities, his behavior was swept under the rug, along with all the victims. Until the king started to take notice about the slaves that were killed by the Baron and his son. Vere may have helped that discovery take place.

He was currently waiting in a receiving room at the palace. It had white plaster walls, red carpet and a pair of wingback chairs. A small fireplace marked one end of the room, and a door the other. The chamber was positively tiny for the large building, but it was intimate, and jammed in a relatively unused aspect of the palace. It ensured privacy as a result.

Vere figured that the king had finally read his report. If so, that would be quite quick of the monarch. It wasn't that King Johan was lazy, it was just that he was busy, and he found spy reports rather boring, unless there was some sort of intrigue associated with them. Vere's stay in Skarva had been largely uneventful, however, and lacked the drama the king enjoyed. He had heard rumblings that the Duchess of Ravens – one of the four leaders of Skarva – was planning a trip to Pinton, but that was just speculation. He'd believe it when he saw her staying in the city.

The door to the small chamber opened, and King Johan swept into the room in a cloud of elegant cologne. He was dressed in a red silk suit with a white shirt, and his long black hair was tied back. King Johan was one of the best-looking men Vere had ever seen, but he had no interest in his monarch in that way. For one, Johan was a king, and two, he was fickle in his interests when it came to romance. And then there was three: Vere had somehow set his sights on a prickly city guard.

Not that he'd done anything about pursuing her. He hadn't wanted to frighten her. She'd suffered enough. He'd take his time. After all, he had plenty of it – at least until he was reassigned. Although, his plan hadn't stopped him thinking a little too much about the quick kiss he'd stolen on the corner of Rock Street.

"Vere."

He stood and bowed to King Johan. Nodding, Johan sat down in the free chair and indicated Vere should return to his seat.

Johan's bright purple eyes met Vere's pale ones. "Vere, I have a favor to ask."

"A favor?" Not that he'd say no, but he did like to know what he was getting into.

"The city guards have approached me recently about a set of abductions."

"Kidnappings?" A leaden feeling took hold in his limbs.

"Yes, apparently women have been taken from all over the city over the last one hundred years. Usually street urchins, or prostitutes, so no one bothered to lodge missing person's reports. But a city guard was abducted six months ago, and she managed to survive. Since then, another girl was taken, but her body was found this week with injuries matching that of the guard's. The City Guard, as a result, has pieced together that vampires are kidnapping girls, torturing them, using them for blood, and then killing them. They hadn't connected all the events because the bodies don't appear regularly or in the same place. And it's over such a long period of time."

The only reason they had managed to link the crimes was because of Billie. Violent deaths happened all the time in Pinton. One body would probably be much like another to the guards, who had more than their fair share to deal with.

"So what is the favor?" Vere asked.

"I want you to look into these deaths. The City Guard think that one of the culprits is educated, or possibly even an aristo. I do not want word of this getting to the papers if that's true."

"What happens if I find them?" Vere asked. He looked down at his nails. He knew what he wanted to do the scumbags who did this.

"Make sure they understand they have to stop."

Vere raised both eyebrows. "That's it?"

He'd always thought the king gave his aristos a fairly loose leash, but this was...it wasn't right. People shouldn't be tortured just for the fun of it. Food was food. If you killed to eat, the death should be quick and clean. And living in Pinton, there was no need to kill humans to survive.

King Johan's expression turned hard. "Then make sure they stop. I do not need any more dramas at the moment. Aristos are screaming bloody murder because of the attempted killing of the Kipling boy and his Chosen. I don't need to give them anything else to complain about."

Kevin's great-aunt had been behind the attempted murders; apparently, she'd taken umbrage at the fact her granddaughter had been Chosen. Vere had been trying to learn more details about the incident, but so far he was out of luck, and Kevin was long gone.

"So I can stop the kidnappers by any means necessary?" Vere asked.

The king stood and walked to the door. "Any means."

"Do you have copies of the case files?"

"I'll have them brought to you before you go."

At least he'd finally learn what Billie's surname was. "Can I seek help from the guards?"

"I'd prefer it if you didn't."

King Johan opened the door and left. They still hadn't talked about his notes.

Chapter Eleven

Billie stepped down the stairs at the City Guard building with care. It was a cold day, and her hip was aching something fierce. She was even tempted to catch a hackney home, and on her wage, that was an extravagance she should probably do without.

As her foot touched the last stair, a low voice reached her. "Morning."

She knew who it was, that baritone had been invading her dreams. Billie took Vere in. He was even better looking than she remembered. His shiny brown hair hung loose over his shoulders, his coat once again hiding his well-muscled body. "Fancy seeing you here."

"Now why would I detect so much sarcasm in that statement?" The corner of his mouth quirked.

Billie's cab ride home was off the cards. She limped down Pittbrough Street toward Marcus Drive. Vere fell into step beside her, his hands clasped behind his back.

"I have no idea," Billie said. It was early morning,

so the street was fairly clear. They could easily walk side-by-side without an issue. Walking next to him didn't feel strange. In fact, it felt right.

"I've been thinking about you," Vere said.

She wasn't about to bite on that lure. "Okay."

"I wanted to see you again, but I wasn't sure if you'd be keen."

Neither was she. In fact, Billie didn't know what she wanted when it came to Vere. Casual sex for her was out of the question. She didn't think she could let someone get that close to her without her heart being engaged. Not after what had happened to her. It took a level of trust to allow someone see her so vulnerable.

Vere shot her a questioning look. "Your silence isn't helping my ego here."

"Sorry, I don't really have an answer for you."

"I thought so. So how about this?" Vere turned to face her. "I help you find the assholes who hurt you."

Billie laughed, but she saw that Vere was dead serious. "Vere…"

"I have connections, Billie. I can help you." He stepped closer, his expression earnest.

"But–"

"For example, I know that another girl was found recently. She had injuries much the same as yours. But she didn't survive."

"That's confidential information."

"I can help."

"I already have the guards."

"But they don't have access into aristo circles."

That was true.

No! She shouldn't even be thinking of going along with his silly plan. He could get hurt.

His eyes burned. "Let me buy you dinner, and I'll tell you how useful I can be."

Why he was so interested in her case, she wondered. Maybe it was just an excuse so he could ask her on a date?

"You can buy me a meal, but I'm not going to discuss confidential issues on the case." Billie tucked her free hand into her jacket pocket, curling her fingers into a loose fist.

*

Billie sat with Vere in a small restaurant that didn't seem to have any specific theme. It felt expensive, and she assumed Vere was paying again. Which made her feel guilty. She wasn't used to having people pay her way. Billie believed in looking after herself, but she didn't earn the kind of money that allowed her to visit places like this all that often. Especially after she'd had to take so much time off work recovering from her injuries.

Vere had asked for a table tucked in the front corner, with a view out the window. The cobblestone street and unlit ornate metal lamps were visible, the sidewalks swept clean of dirt. Stone buildings arched toward the sky, which was pinkening with dawn. Vendors who'd catered for the vampire crowd were closing down for the day, their bright canvas overhangs being rolled up and tucked away.

Turning her attention back inside, her gaze rested

on the pink and white checkered tablecloth, white napkins and sparkling glassware. She couldn't see a menu. It was time to confront the truth: she was infatuated with a human aristo. What she didn't understand was what he saw in *her*. A battered and beat up version of her former self. She might have passed for pretty, back before her body had been covered in scars from years of guard work, and then the attack that should have killed her.

Vere flicked his napkin out with a snap, then smoothed it over his lap. "So, how many victims did you work out there'd been?"

Billie copied his gesture, but with much less finesse. "That's confidential."

If he'd been a vampire, she'd have worried he was trying to work out how much she knew, and if she was a potential threat. But at least she knew he wasn't one of the kidnappers – he was human. Plus, she'd never forget the way her attackers sounded, nor the way the aristo had smelled. Cucumber and rose.

And Vere smelt like coffee and whiskey.

"Look, I can help you, Billie."

"I'm sure you can." She gave him one of her 'city guard' smiles. The one she did to placate someone. Billie didn't bother trying to soothe ruffled feathers in her personal life. Oh wait, she didn't *have* a personal life.

He frowned at her. "I'm serious."

"So am I."

She had a feeling he wasn't about to let it go. And really, unless he went to the papers – and she seriously doubted an aristo would lower himself to that level – was there any harm in telling him? Vere seemed like he wanted to help her, not hinder her. Maybe he *could* ask questions she wasn't able to.

And maybe she was trusting the wrong person. But she'd never know unless she tried.

"Fine."

The waiter arrived then. "What would you like to order?"

She hadn't even seen a menu. Vere sighed. "What is available?"

The waiter rattled off a list of items that she found impressive. The memory, not the food. They could do with someone like that at the guards. The waiter was a woman, five feet nothing, and skinny as a stick. But she could be trained. It depended on whether she wanted a career bashing skulls or taking down food orders.

The waiter levelled her cool brown eyes on Billie. "Your order, madam?"

Right. Quickly, she ran back through the list, and said, "The pasta."

The waiter turned to Vere. "A coffee. And a piece of your cake of the day." When Billie looked at him, he gave her an elegant shrug. "It's too late for a real meal." He winked. Aristos tended to kept night hours, like her, she figured. "And it's not chocolate cake."

Late. Right. It was morning for Billie. And morning equaled dinner time. Gah.

Chapter Twelve

"There's been at least six victims a year, for a hundred years," Billie said.

Vere leaned back slightly. Over *six hundred* humans had been kidnapped, beaten and then killed? And no one had noticed? "How has this gone undetected?"

Billie fiddled with the edge of the napkin in her lap, her eyes downcast. He wanted her to look at him. "Aside from their injuries, very little links the victims. Age, sex, height, weight, skin color – they all vary. The dump sites for the bodies are different as well: the Thyme, back alleys, blood dens, and garbage barges. And the disposal of the bodies occurs randomly throughout the year. Some of the victims are reported as missing, but most aren't. They normally select individuals who won't be missed."

Vere imagined this is what a headache felt like. These criminals had been operating for over one hundred years and no one had figured it out. Vampires didn't *get* headaches.

"Well, we know the perpetrators are at least one hundred years old – probably more like one hundred and fifty." Vere placed a palm on the linen-covered table.

"I'd gathered that much."

"Yes, but at least that will narrow down the search a little." He'd have to do some research at the palace in the records office, but he could track down the vampires with birth records past then. Although, that left *him* on the prospective killers list. At least he knew he wasn't guilty.

The young waiter appeared, with Vere's coffee and cake, and Billie's pasta. The rich aroma of garlic, basil and tomato reached him. A glass of wine was placed next to her dish. The city guard frowned at the alcohol. "I didn't order a wine."

The waiter nodded slightly. "It's complimentary with the dish." Then the thin woman turned away to serve another table.

Vere glanced at the glass then Billie. "You don't drink?" He took a sip of his coffee. Hot and strong. Just the way he liked it.

She sighed. "I do, but not when I'm on duty."

"Haven't you finished your shift?" He'd thought she was on her way home.

"Yes."

"Then you're not on duty."

"But we're talking work."

"Unofficially." He gave her a large smile. She blinked then took a sip of the wine, almost out of reflex. He hoped it meant she was impressed by his expression, rather than alarmed by it.

Billie reached down and picked up her cutlery. "Mind if I start?"

He waved a hand in the air. "By all means." He picked up a fork and cut away a piece of cake. He wasn't really hungry, but he wanted to set her at ease.

Delicately, she began to eat her meal. She must have been starving, he thought, since it was the end of her shift, but she maintained utter control. He noticed she kept flicking glances his way, like she was gauging his reaction. He took another sip of coffee to make it look like he wasn't paying attention.

The silence stretched between them as she ate, and he found it soothing. He didn't mind just being *with* her, her intensity and personality enough. Oh boy, he was in trouble.

Once she finished the last morsel of food, and he had eaten his cake, he propped his elbows on the table. "Good?"

She wiped the corners of her mouth with her napkin, his eyes snagging on the scar on her neck as he followed the cloth's journey back to her lap.

An almost wistful expression marked her face. "Wonderful. How was your dessert?"

"Good." It was some type of vanilla-flavored sponge cake. The coffee was better.

Vere figured she must not get to eat out very often. At least not at venues like this. He wondered how much a city guard earned. It couldn't be that bad. But then, eating out at restaurants wasn't exactly a cheap hobby.

Beckoning the waiter over, Vere asked for the check. The waiter returned with the bill marked on a small slip of paper. Vere paid in cash, and as they were leaving, Billie turned to the woman. "If you ever want to change careers, your memory would be an asset at the city guards. Think about it." Nodding, she left. The waitress stared at Billie's back, her mouth slightly agape.

On the street, Vere felt the weak warmth of the day radiating through his cloak. "You said there were two attackers? Did they seem organized?"

Billie glanced up at the sun, her eyes squinting in the light. She shivered and started walking. "Yes."

"Do you think there were any more?" He caught up with her.

Shaking her head, her brown braid swayed with the movement. He wanted to run his fingers over the silky strands. This was getting a little out of control.

"No. But the guy who grabbed me – I thought that was the one in charge. But on the last day, I realized that he wasn't. He was just the muscle. It was the aristo who called the shots." Billie looked over at him out the corner of her eye. "I'll never forget the sound of their voices."

Vere hoped that the next time she heard them, it would be the sound of their screams.

Chapter Thirteen

Two days had passed since Vere had asked her to dinner. And she hadn't seen hide nor hair of him. She didn't know whether to be pissed off or relieved. He'd said he wanted to help her, but she wasn't sure what kind of help an aristo human could provide. And he hadn't kissed her again.

Argh. She was turning herself into a ninnyhammer.

Billie wasn't the kind of woman to sit and wait for a man to show interest in her, but she didn't really have the courage to approach him, either. He was so far away from her on the social food-chain that she may as well be trying to reach for the stars.

You should be focusing on the case, she lectured herself.

In fact, that's what she'd been doing before she started daydreaming about shiny brown hair, pale gray eyes and those lips. Going over the other files was why she'd refused an invitation to go out drinking with the other guards, after all. Not that she was sure they'd wanted her there anyway. Well, Oliver and Kyle would have. But not the others. They felt uncomfortable around her.

Pulling herself back to reality, she stared at the wooden dining table that sat in the center of her apartment. Her flat was a small one-roomed affair, with a kitchenette to her left, and a bed to her right. A small door led off into a bathroom that contained a shower, chipped sink and toilet. The water was cold as often as it was hot. But it was home.

Back in the day, she would have spread all her paperwork on the wooden floor – more room – but getting down to ground level and climbing back up was too much effort now. Yellow-colored files were spread out before her on the table, with others in piles on the floor, and she thumbed through one. Alice's neat handwriting only covered four of the autopsies Billie had read. Alice had been working on her own as the coroner for a year now, and before that, had been the assistant to Dr. Botham. The former coroner's script was present on over three hundred of the case files.

Part of Billie wanted to find Botham and clobber him over the head. How had he missed the connections? Alice had managed to join the dots within her first year on the job. If he had noticed something sooner, hundreds of people might still be alive. *She* wouldn't have been abducted.

As she leaned down to grab the topmost file off the pile, a knock sounded at her door. If she was quiet, maybe whoever it was would think she wasn't home. Billie's apartment was on the ground floor – which had worked out well, considering she had the place before she'd been injured – and sometimes the hawkers who managed to make it into the building would target her and her neighbors before they were kicked out.

Holding her breath, she waited for thirty seconds.

The knock sounded again.

Frowning, she heaved herself up and limped toward the door. Maybe it was one of her neighbors come to borrow a cup of sugar or something. Mrs. Arrowny three doors down loved to bake. Not that Billie had something as pricey as a cup of sugar on hand.

Opening the door, Billie spotted Vere on her doorstep. Peering around him, she saw nobody else in the stone hallway. "How did you get in here?"

Vere tucked a strand of hair behind his ear. "One of your neighbors let me in."

Billie narrowed her eyes. "Which one?"

He gave her that familiar half-grin. "I'm not saying, because you look like you might want to hurt them for it."

"Great."

"Can I come in?"

Billie opened her mouth to say no. She'd made it clear that she hadn't wanted him to know where she lived, but he'd managed to track her down anyway. He hadn't seemed like the type of guy to be a stalker, but it appeared she was wrong.

"The time you're taking to think this over is worrying me." Vere's smile disappeared.

"Fine." Billie stepped back to give him enough

room to pass.

She shut the door with a click. Vere had stopped just inside the doorway and was looking around her apartment. He made her home feel tiny. Embarrassment swamped her. Sure, her place was on the small side, but at least it was clean and relatively neat – except for the piles and piles of folders surrounding her table. He didn't have to make her feel like she was living in a dive. Just because it wasn't an estate.

Rather than yell at him like she wanted to, Billie took a deep breath and counted to ten. "Take a seat."

Vere shrugged his greatcoat off and hung it over the back of one of her three chairs. He then took the seat she'd been sitting on.

"First and foremost," Billie said, limping closer. "How did you find out where I live?"

Chapter Fourteen

Vere had a feeling that he was in Billie's bad books. The dark scowl she wore gave that away. But it wasn't like he'd stalked her to learn her address – it had been in one of the case files that the king had given him. Although, he might have been looking for it when he went over the documents.

"I managed to get copies of the reports," Vere gave a nonchalant shrug. "It was in there."

Billie's expression turned thunderous. "You got *copies* of the reports?" She stomped over to the table and pulled out a chair. She collapsed rather than eased herself onto it and rubbed her hip. It must be bothering her.

He tried to look around in a discreet fashion. He wanted to know all about the woman in front of him, and people's homes often reflected their personalities. The apartment was tidy, not necessarily spotless, but that didn't matter. There was nothing on the floor, aside from the stacks of reports, and minimal decorations. It was austere. The air smelled strongly of lemons and Billie. He wanted to inhale the scent deeply, but had a feeling it would make him appear even more suspect in her mind.

Dark brown eyes stared at him. "How did you get copies of the reports?"

Vere raised his hands, palms facing her. "I can't divulge my sources."

"Can't or won't?"

He sighed. "Both."

Vere didn't think that the king would be happy if he announced to Billie that their fair monarch was the leak. After all, the king hadn't really wanted Vere to contact the City Guard. And he hadn't. Not officially. That's how he was going to argue the situation, anyway, if King Johan asked. Which he doubted he would, provided the killers were found and the whole 'mess' was sorted out nicely.

Billie clasped her hands together and rested them on top of one of the yellow folders. "You make it really hard to trust you, you know that, right?"

He was a spy.

He wasn't really all that trustworthy.

Oh wait, she didn't know that.

"Look, I'd love to tell you, but I'd like my head to stay exactly where it is. That's all."

Exasperation oozed out of her pores. "Why are you here?"

He wanted to kiss her. Well, do more than kiss her.

Everything about the woman appealed to him. It was dangerous, for her and him. He couldn't risk starting a relationship with her, because if she found out he was a vampire, she might stake him. Or hate him. He wasn't sure which ending was worse. But Vere wanted to know what it would be like to be with *her*. He'd never met anyone, man or woman, who could hold a candle to her inner strength.

"I wanted to talk over the case with you. See if you can remember anything from where you were held. If I can track down the property, then that would help us work out who the killers might be."

"It was dark, and I was kept in a basement. I couldn't really hear the sound of anything, and there were no windows. Not even boarded up, because boards usually let in a little light."

Vere tapped his fingers against his thigh. That could be any of hundreds of houses in the city. *Great.* He saw Billie's eyes drop down to his lap and his hand. He wanted to make a joke, but then he noticed her expression. Fatigue. Weariness. And hunger.

Vere closed some of the distance between them. "Billie…"

Almost against her will, she moved closer to him too. "Yes?" Her voice was a little breathy. So maybe she *had* enjoyed their kiss. He sure had.

Lowering his voice, he murmured, "I know your surname."

She laughed. It was full and throaty and just about floored him. Her scar stood out on her throat, but he couldn't pay attention to it. His gaze was drawn to her lips, and teeth, and the joy that suffused her expression. He wanted to make her laugh again.

"Billie?"

She looked at him, mirth still dancing in her eyes. "Yes?"

His fingers playing with dark strands of hair that had fallen from her braid. "I'm going to kiss you now."

*

Billie froze, like a deer caught in a hunter's sight. But she didn't pull away. She couldn't. Vere moved toward her, slowly, giving her enough time to say no. And then his mouth touched hers. He still tasted like coffee and whiskey. Was that all he ate? Couldn't be, he was too muscular to live on a diet of booze and caffeine.

His lips were warm and firm, and gentle. He took his time, and for a few moments, Billie was content with him leading the way. But she wasn't a pushover, and had never been the kind of woman to sit back and be taken for a ride. With a small moan, she pressed her torso against Vere's, and brushed her tongue along his lips. They parted with a small gasp, and she swept inside.

A groan reverberated through the room, and Vere pulled back, resting his forehead against hers. "Billie, I know it's only a kiss, but you're killing me."

She chuckled. She actually chuckled. Being near Vere made her feel powerful and strong, like her near-death hadn't happened. He just accepted her for who and what she was, no questions asked. For the first time since she woke up in that hospital bed, she felt beautiful. Desirable. "Come now," she joked, "I thought aristos were harder to kill than that."

His gray eyes developed a wicked gleam. "Oh,

we're hard all right."

"Really?" Her palm itched to find out for itself. *You're mad.*

"Mmmhhmm."

"Vere?"

His eyes dropped to her mouth. "Yes?"

"Can we kiss a little more?" Her voice had a teasing husky quality that didn't belong to her.

His deep baritone washed over her. "Only if you don't mind me doing a little more than kissing."

She bit her lip. "But you'll stop if I ask?"

He drew back, and she felt the loss of his warmth, his strength. He was frowning at her, all traces of mirth gone. "Of course. What kind of a man do you think I am?"

Billie gave a faint smile. "A nice one?"

He was kind to her, and patient, but she still didn't *know* him very well. But for some reason, she trusted him. That he would keep her best interests at heart, even in this.

"Nice." His expression radiated disbelief.

"Nice."

"No man wants to be called *nice*." He said it almost as if she'd cussed him out.

"What's wrong with it?" Women were called nice all the time. Although, never her. Forthright. Strong-minded. Decisive. That was before she was abducted. After that it was tough, brave, and courageous. Just for living her everyday life, like she needed a medal for surviving.

"Boys are nice. Men aren't nice."

"Then what are they?"

"Manly. Sexy. Virile."

Billie couldn't help smirking. "Virile?"

Vere nodded. "Who wouldn't want to be called virile?"

Billie raised both eyebrows. "Me."

"But you aren't a man."

"Thank you for noticing." She poked her tongue out.

He tapped his fingers again. "Billie, can we kiss some more? Or do we need to discuss my manhood a bit further?"

Hooking a finger in the collar of his no doubt very expensive shirt, she tugged Vere closer to her. "What are you waiting for?"

CHAPTER FIFTEEN

What had she done?

Nothing a normal adult wouldn't have, Billie told herself.

But what had she *done*?

She was lying in her bed, on her side under the pale blue quilt, snuggled up next to an aristo. The weak afternoon sunlight that filtered through her blinds bathed them in a soft radiance. She was out of her bloody mind, who cares what she'd done. The smooth skin of Vere's chest felt like the most comfortable pillow she'd ever had. If anything, the utter peace and quiet she felt with him was worse.

She *cared* about him.

You barely know him.

And that was the problem. She knew his name, where he lived, that he preferred *coffee* over *chocolate*, that he was an aristo – probably a second or third son – and that he was ridiculously good in bed. But she didn't know what his favorite color was, or what his family members' names were, or even how old he was.

He could be married, for all she knew.

Oh, please don't let him be married.

Billie knew aristos lived different lifestyles to people of lower classes, and that marriage was a contractual thing, rather than something about emotion. But middle-class people like her tried to marry for love. She couldn't handle being the 'other person'.

You should have just said 'no.'

But she hadn't wanted to. Not at all. It made her tingle all over just remembering the way his lips had felt against hers, the heat and pleasure of his hands moving over her…

"Want to go another round?"

Billie tilted her face to look at him. "What?"

The smooth lines of his jaw showed a day-old growth, and his face was even prettier up close. He ran a hand over his chin, as if thinking hard. "I think I could try one more time."

Billie snuggled back against Vere. A giggle wound its way up through her, but she clamped it down and started drawing little circles over his stomach. He had washboard abs, with a thin line of dark hair marking a path down below the covers. How many aristos had a stomach like that? "You are *so* romantic."

She could feel him speak, as much as she could hear the words. "You want romance?"

"Doesn't everyone?" Although, she'd never really thought she was the kind of person who'd be into it. But what do you know? A handsome man wore her down, climbed into bed with her, rocked her socks off, and then propositioned her with a deadpan offer. Hrm. Turns out, she wanted a bit more than that.

She shied away from what else she wanted.

He pushed himself up, and Billie fell back onto her own pillow. Placing one hand over his heart, he stared deep into her eyes. "I want to make sweet love to you under the afternoon sunshine. Your beauty makes me weep. I cannot contain myself to just one sampling of your generous charms…"

Billie couldn't help herself. She laughed.

"What? You wanted romance. Or do you want me to get down on my knees and beg for one more chance to woo your lovely–"

She threw her pillow at him. It hit him straight in the face, and he let out an *oomph*. She figured he could have probably caught the missile, but when he pulled the pillow away he was grinning. "Oh, so you want to turn this into a challenge?"

Then he pounced. Pinning her underneath him, his hair created a silk curtain that enclosed the two of them. Billie shook her head. "No challenge. I need to go to work."

He frowned. "Work?"

"Work."

"But–"

"Work."

"Two minutes?"

Laughter burst out of her. "Two minutes may be enough for you, but not for me."

"Come on, two minutes of sex is better than no minutes of sex."

"Maybe for a guy," Billie said.

Vere rolled away, onto his back. "You wound me."

"Come on, move your aristo butt."

Billie climbed out of the bed, suddenly conscious of her scars. *He's seen them anyway.* Pulling on her clothing from its pile on the floor next to her bed, she tried not to think about what had happened. Not too much. She didn't want to get her hopes up.

When she turned back to face Vere, he was already dressed, and looked like he hadn't spent the afternoon rolling around on a bed with a city guard. Hair immaculately tied back, clothes righted, he looked like he'd just stepped out of a luncheon.

"Can you remember anything else about your attackers? Their voices, the room, anything?"

Her good mood dropped. So he was serious about wanting to help find her kidnappers. She inhaled deeply, keeping her expression neutral. But that just highlighted Vere's coffee and whiskey smell – something that suited him. Unlike her attacker, with his fake cologne.

"Nothing I haven't told you already." Billie walked over to the door, and grabbed her scarf off one of the pegs that hung near the entryway. Wrapping it around her throat, she paused. "Except that the boss guy smelled like cucumber and roses."

Chapter Sixteen

Cucumber and roses.

The description nagged at Vere. It wasn't a common scent for a vampire – they didn't tend to wear strong colognes. Mostly because something that could be smelt by a human was probably overpowering to a vampire. But Billie had noticed it.

He climbed up the stairs of his father's townhouse and then quietly let himself in the large front doors. The less his family knew of his movements, the better. He would have come in via the rear door, but his father had heard of him doing that before, and the lecture on propriety hadn't been worth the attempted secrecy of his movements.

White plaster walls soared high overhead, with expensive paintings of aristos adorning their surfaces. The cold eyes of his ancestors stared into the hall, condescension etched on their features. Each one of them had bright purple eyes – his 'weak coloring' as his father put it – came from his mother's side. He didn't like the look of his forebears. They seemed like stuck up assholes. But that was the aristocracy for you.

Vere caught sight of his brother's valet, who was walking up the large staircase to the second floor. The man was limping slightly. Odd, on two counts. One, that a vampire was limping and two, servants were meant to use the rear stairwell.

"Vere!" Vere's father was walking across the black marble floor of the foyer.

The servant high-tailed it up the staircase and down the hallway.

"Father."

Baron Moore preferred to be called 'my lord', even by his offspring. His face pinched in annoyance. "Where have you been?"

His father was shorter than Vere, balding, and with a sharp nose that seemed to always be tilted in such a way so that he was looking down on everyone he encountered. Which was a feat, considering the height difference between father and son.

"You smell like a woman." His father's eyes narrowed. "A human woman."

Vere shrugged, flicking an imaginary piece of lint from his sleeve. Then he took a step closer to his parent. "And you smell like cucumber." He sniffed. "And roses."

Vere had never smelled that odor on his father before. He would have remembered it. Then again, Vere had been away for a year. Things could change in that time. But he certainly hadn't picked the scent up in the house since he'd returned.

"It's your brother's cologne," Baron Moore

replied, defensive. Few vampires wore cologne. Half of society frowned on it, and the other half didn't care one way or the other. The Baron was a socialite if ever there was one – other people's opinions mattered. Just not Vere's. Normally.

"It's an odd scent, I know," the Baron continued. "But your brother just purchased a new bottle – he has it specially made – and I was out of mine. I have to duck out to a dinner with Earl of Milton and Viscountess Kipling, and I couldn't risk just smelling like soap."

His brother got the cologne specially made. His father could be lying, but then, why would he? The Baron would have no idea that it was the only real thing that Billie could remember about her attacker. And he wouldn't care even if he did know – humans meant nothing to the other aristo. Less than that, since he couldn't own slaves anymore.

Hadn't been allowed to in a little over a hundred years.

Vere shifted his stance slightly, to appear casual. He hoped that he was hiding the fact that he wanted to strangle his brother to death. Maybe bludgeon him a bit first. With his own limb. "Do you know where Bryce is now?"

"No." Baron Moore shrugged. "He and his valet went out somewhere. I hope he isn't out blowing his allowance again. He does love to play it a bit rough in those blood dens. I've lost track of how many fines I've had to pay for him; he gets excitable with some of the blood whores from time to time."

Vere's stomach dropped. He swallowed back a

surge of bile. "His valet returned."

"Ask him where Bryce has gone then. I don't want to be late."

Vere's instinct was screaming at him to run out the door, check on Billie, make sure she was okay. But she was just going to the City Guard office. She would be walking down public streets and it was late afternoon – she'd be safe. It was harder to kidnap someone in broad daylight. Plus, if he found the valet, then he could track down Bryce. And then he wouldn't have to worry about the valet warning his brother.

Chapter Seventeen

Billie's first thought when she opened her eyes was *not again.*

Her head was pounding. Lifting a hand to touch the lump she could feel on the back of her skull, she met resistance. Her wrists were chained together.

Billie tried to assess the situation, tried to fight back the growing panic that was causing her heart to beat faster, her breath to pant, and making her want to scream. *You will be okay,* she told herself. *You survived once, you will do it again.*

She was only lying to herself.

There were only two people who would want to kidnap her again, and they would ensure that she really was dead this time.

Just assess the situation, work out your escape route.

Billie almost laughed. She was on her back, cold stone pressing against her shoulder blades and butt, and she knew she'd have bruises tomorrow. *If* she survived, she'd have bruises tomorrow. The room was dark, except for the lone candle that flickered in one corner. It illuminated a stone wall, and a girl slumped against it. So Billie wasn't alone this time.

The girl's arms were secured above her head, steel chains and cuffs looped through an eyehook located several yards above her head. Her hair was long and blonde and so matted with filth and blood she would have to shave it if she ever managed to escape. Her clothes were tatters around her body, and her skin was stretched thin over bones, visible through the materials' rips and tears. Vampire bites covered almost every spare inch of observable flesh.

If the girl lived, she'd be completely bit-ridden.

Billie blinked once, twice, hoping that this was just another nightmare. But the same images were visible when she re-opened her eyes both times. How had she been caught? She remembered walking down Pittbrough Street, mere blocks from the office, when a black carriage had pulled up alongside her. Someone had thrown a hessian bag over her head, and she'd started to scream, flailing with her cane. But then there'd been a burst of agony radiating out from her skull and everything went dim.

"You're awake again."

Billie's gaze flicked around the room, trying to find the source of the speaker. The smooth tones told her it was the aristo, not the hired muscle, who was talking. "Very observant."

The vampire let out a short bark of laughter, and stepped into the light of the candle. He wore a white singlet, black breeches and knee-high boots. His mouse-brown hair was tied back in a queue, and his eyes were the bright violet that she expected to see on an aristo leech. There was something familiar in the angle of his jaw, but she couldn't be sure. Maybe she just wanted there to be a familiarity to him – so that she'd remember his face when she killed him.

Hah.

Aren't I hilarious?

"I didn't care that you'd survived your little swim in the river. What marvelous news it made: the amazing city guard who thwarted death. How heroic. What strength." He clapped slowly. "If you'd just left it alone, everything would have been fine. But then you came knocking on the door of my estate."

Billie frowned. "When was I at your estate?"

She'd only been to one estate recently, and that was Vere's. But he was human. And this aristo was *definitely* a vampire.

"Mmm. I didn't believe my valet at first. What were you doing at *my* house? How could you have found me? But then I saw you for myself. Sitting out to dinner with my *brother*. Your scar out for the world to see."

Billie swallowed, rage building within her with every word the man uttered. "I haven't been anywhere with your *brother*."

The aristo laughed. The girl next to him started, then looked up with dreamy brown eyes. She was still high from a bite. The vampire ran a finger over her cheek, almost lover-like. Billie wanted to puke.

"Oh, you've done a lot more than simply eat dinner with my brother." The aristo took a few steps closer, his face cast in shadow as he moved away from the candle's luminescence.

He's lying.

"Nothing to say to that?" He leaned down over her, blocking the little light in the room. She wanted to inch away, but there was nowhere to go.

Billie spat.

He jerked back, cursing. Then a foot slammed into her side. Billie screamed, she couldn't stop herself, pain exploding in her ribs. Breathing became impossible, and she curled into a fetal position, as much as the chains would allow. A fist grabbed her hair, jerking her head back.

She could barely open her eyes. Billie had to stay alert, to stay alive. The guards would find her. Vere would find her. She didn't know how, but he would.

"You stink of my brother, you fucking whore. Did you fuck him to find out more information about me?"

"I don't even know who your brother is," Billie gritted. She didn't *know* any vampires. The scent of cucumbers and rose wafted over to her.

The leech slammed her head against the stone floor. Sharp pain burst behind her eyes, and she fought to stay conscious. Breathe, just breathe, she told herself.

The aristo snarled. "When I'm done with you, you'll wish you hadn't survived. But think on the bright side – when I'm done, Vere and I can compare notes on the kind of fuck you are."

Vere.

No.

Vere had gray eyes. *Or eyes so light a purple they could be gray.* That's what she'd first thought. How could she have missed that he was a vampire? He ate and drank. He seemed normal.

"Vere will kill you," Billie said, fighting for calm. Inside, though, she was screaming at what an utter idiot she'd been.

Vere is a vampire.

He'd wanted inside information on the case.

His brother was her abductor.

Vere had been just using her. And she'd let him. She'd *trusted* him. Maybe she didn't deserve to live. Not if she was that stupid. Maybe the leech was right.

"Now." The aristo let go of her hair. "Let's get properly reacquainted."

CHAPTER EIGHTEEN

The valet was nowhere to be found.

It didn't matter though. There was only one place that Bryce could have gone – he was too cheap to rent new accommodations for himself, and the family had a small warehouse on the other side of the Thyme River. The building had a basement.

But first, Vere had to check that Billie was okay.

Striding up the City Guard steps, he burst through the double doors and into the reception area. A large, burly looking guard looked up from behind the solid metal counter, sheets of paper in the human's big hands. A man dressed like a cit – a wealthy businessman – was on the other side of the high desk, gesticulating wildly.

Vere came to a stop next to the cit. "I need to speak to someone in charge. Now."

The guard looked at him. The man was as tall, if not a bit taller, than Vere. The guy's dark skin had a few scars on its surface – war wounds, no doubt – and he wore a no-nonsense expression. "Wait your turn."

Vere didn't care for the guard's attitude. "I need to see someone immediately."

The cit sneered at him. Vere committed the human's face to memory. Medium height, slim build, olive skin and brown eyes. The man might end up with a bruised face someday, if he went down the wrong street, or entered the wrong club.

The city guard waved some papers at him. "Look, I have someone with me right now."

Vere leaned on the desk, urgency layering his voice. "I need to know if Billie Young showed up for work."

The human tapped the counter. "Hello? You were dealing with *my* issue."

"Wait a second." The guard ducked into the backroom, and Vere could hear him ask where Billie was. Silence. Then an even larger human man came out from the rear room. His midnight-black skin shone in the gas lamps, and his gaze was serious as he looked at Vere.

"You're asking about Billie?" The man's voice was a deep rumble, and Vere instantly liked him. He couldn't pinpoint why, and he honestly didn't care.

"Has she shown up at work today?" Vere was losing his patience.

"What's Billie to you?"

"For fuck's sake. Is she here or not?"

"No."

Vere turned to bolt. She was meant to have left her apartment soon after he'd gone. She should have been here by now. "Fuck!"

A hand grabbed his arm. Vere looked down. "If

you don't let me go, you'll lose your limb."

Concern marked the huge man's expression. "Do you know where she is?"

"I hope I'm wrong, but I think so."

"Do you think she's hurt?"

Vere nodded, his throat dry. "Worse."

Fire lit the man's eyes. "Tell me where you're going, we'll meet you there."

CHAPTER NINETEEN

She didn't know how many bones in her body were broken now. Vere's brother had decided to use her as a punching bag and breathing was more than a challenge. But he'd needed a 'rest' and so had vanished into the darkness of the room. But Billie knew he was still there. The chained girl had watched, wearing a goofy smile the whole time. Even though Billie knew the other human was drugged out of her mind, she still wanted to wipe the expression off her face. With her fists.

Vere's brother strode into the candlelight. Raising one of his fists to his mouth, he licked her blood off his skin. "Now, wasn't that foreplay fun?"

Maybe for him.

She didn't know how she was still conscious. He'd been careful to avoid hitting her face – so he could look into her eyes when he fucked her, he said – but her body ached with a mixture of burning and stabbing pain. Surely she should have passed out by now?

The leech's hands dropped down to his fly, and he began to unbutton his trousers. He wanted her to be scared. The blonde girl opened her mouth behind him, and Billie didn't want to think what she'd been used for before. Her stomach threatened to revolt.

The vampire's hand froze on the last button. He turned toward the shadows of the room. "You're here already? I told you to give me a few hours."

Then she heard it. A second set of footsteps.

"I didn't realize I was expected at all." That voice. Billie froze, her heart pounding.

"*Vere*?" Confusion sounded in the aristo's voice, and she knew then that Vere wasn't part of this little sick hobby. At least, she hoped he wasn't.

Vere strode into the room, most of his features shadowed, his greatcoat swirling around him. She couldn't see his expression, but his anger was like a physical thing, a pulsing emotion that wreathed through the room. "Bryce," Vere shook his head. "You sick asshole."

"Me? Sick?" Bryce laughed loudly, but his face fell into a look of contempt as he laid his eyes on his brother. "You're the fucking weakling who doesn't like to treat humans like what they are – prey."

"Prey? Yes. But real hunters don't play with their food." Vere's eyes swept the room, and she felt that pale gaze come to rest on her. Fear flashed across his features, but vanished just as quickly. Had she imagined it?

"Oh yes, I managed to grab your latest toy. Doesn't she look pretty now I've gotten her ready?" Bryce rubbed his chin.

Billie wanted to slit his throat. Then stab the bastard in the eye.

Vere didn't seem to listen. "You need to stop this. Now. Forever. Or I'll stop it for you." Now Vere smiled, an even, unhurried expression.

Bryce moved closer to him. Away from her, and the girl. "You've got to be kidding me." Disbelief drenched Bryce's voice. "I'm not going to stop. And you're not going to tell the guards or anyone about it. Imagine the scandal for the family, if I got arrested. None of the vampires would care why, mind you, they'd just be horrified by the fact that I managed to get caught. You wouldn't be able to travel anymore; father would be banned from his clubs."

Vere nodded, dropping his greatcoat to the floor, then kicking it away into the darkness. "I was hoping you'd say something like that."

"Really?" Bryce's expression brightened.

"Yes." Vere smiled, a toothy expression. His fangs were visible.

Oh, she was a *moron*.

"Because I was told to ensure all this," Vere waved a hand, indicating the room, the girl, *her*, "stops, by any means necessary."

Bryce laughed. "Told? By who?"

"The king."

"The king told you to catch *me*?"

"The kidnapper. Which happens to be you."

"As if the king told you–"

Vere *moved*. So fast, she couldn't follow the exact movements, but he whipped out a series of kicks and punches that had Bryce ducking and weaving. A number of thuds told Billie every time Vere made contact.

"That all you got?" Bryce spat a glob of blood on the floor. "You won't be able to kill me with a few hits."

"That's why I brought this." Vere pulled out a long, fire-hardened knife from behind his back.

"You got *wood*?"

Billie wanted to laugh at the phrasing, but she just lay there, immobile. She saw the exact moment Bryce decided to run, but Vere simply moved a little to his left and tripped his brother. Bryce caught himself before he fell, but Vere grabbed him and threw him into a wall. He followed his brother's body, launching another series of kicks and punches. By the time Bryce pulled himself back up, he was sporting cuts over his arms and chest. Vere kicked out, thrusting with the blade of his foot into Bryce's knee. The crunching of bone echoed in the room.

Bryce fell to the floor with a howl. "Why?" he panted.

"So how do we do this? Billie?" Vere didn't look at her, his attention consumed by his brother. "Was it a broken arm and hip?"

"Hip, then arm," Billie said. "You need to stomp on the hip, though."

Vere lifted his foot and then slammed his boot down. More breaking bone and another scream. "Like this?"

"Exactly like that."

"What the fuck, Vere! I'm your *brother*!"

"How'd he break your arm?"

"Pinned my elbow down, then just pulled it up. Vampire strength."

"I see." Vere stood on his brother's forearm, then snapped the long bones. Another yell.

"*Vere!*"

He dragged Bryce over to her, careful to keep his sibling out of her reach. "Do you want to finish it?"

Oh, Billie wanted to scream a yes. But she couldn't move. If she did, she'd die. The pain would kill her. "You do it."

His pale eyes met hers. "Are you sure?"

"No, Vere! I'm your brother, she's just a whore."

Vere's gaze sliced to his sibling. "She is worth one hundred of you."

Bryce spat. "You fucking piece of shit. You would pick a human over me?"

Vere's voice was low, gravelly. "I would pick her over *anyone*."

Billie shut her eyes for a second. Vere hadn't really said that. "Slit his throat first."

"*No!*"

"For you." Then the wooden knife slipped across Bryce' neck, and the skin parted like warm butter. Blood spurted from the wound, splattering Vere. Without flinching, he stabbed the weapon down, into his brother's heart.

CHAPTER TWENTY

Vere's brother was dead.

And Billie wasn't far behind, by the looks of it. Holding back his fear, Vere went to step over Bryce's body when he felt something brush against the back of his neck. Spinning, he saw Bryce's valet, face contorted with rage, a wooden blade of his own in hand.

Vere lunged out the way, but the knife cut into his left bicep. His own weapon was still in his brother's corpse.

Billie screamed. "Vere!"

Moving faster than he thought he could, he danced out of the way of the knife, dodging wild strikes. His opponent was fueled by anger, whereas Vere felt eerily calm. Even when he'd beat his brother to within an inch of his life, he'd felt that battle-serenity descend. It's what he'd trained for over the years. He might be a spy with a largely social role, but he knew how to fight just in case he needed to get himself out of trouble.

Slamming the blade of his hand out, he shattered the wrist of the valet. The wooden knife dropped to the floor and they both dove for it, grappling on the ground. Vere rolled, pinning the other vampire beneath him. Reaching out with his left hand, he managed to swipe up the knife. But his grip loosened on the valet, and the man head-butted him, breaking his nose. Sharp pain shot through his face, and his eyes watered. Blood poured down over his lips.

He had to end this. He sprang to his feet, the valet followed, but too slow. Stepping forward, Vere drove the knife home. The other man gasped, his mouth opening and closing like a fish on land, and then toppled over.

Dropping to his knees, Vere grabbed his nose between finger and thumb and realigned it back into place. His eyes watered again, but his accelerated healing would do the rest. He tore off part of his shirt and used it to bind the wound on his arm; a cut made by a wooden instrument wouldn't mend so quickly.

"Billie?" He was covered in blood – his, Bryce's, the valet's – but then, so was Billie. And it was all her own.

Carefully, he moved her shirt out of the way, so he could see the damage. Even though the room was only illuminated by a single candle, everything held a sharp clarity. Billie's stomach was one massive bruise, parts already turning black. She was probably bleeding internally, not that he knew much about human medicine. But she could die from that.

Billie's faint voice reached him. "You lied to me."

"What?" Her face was largely unmarred, and her

brown eyes stared at him.

"You let me believe you were human."

"I *didn't* say I was human. You never asked." Should they be arguing about this right now?

"Did you know about your brother?"

He shut his eyes. How could she think that? And what could he say? That yes, he knew his brother was a bastard, but no, he didn't know that he'd been kidnapping and killing humans for over a century? What kind of spy did that make him?

"No. I didn't work it out until I got home this morning, and I smelled the cologne."

"Did the king really tell you to stop this?" Her voice was getting weaker.

Vere nodded, leaning closer to her. "He did."

Billie raised her arm then, her fingertips carefully touching his cheek. "Thank you for coming for me."

And then her arm dropped. Her eyes closed. She was barely breathing.

"Billie? Billie!"

He couldn't shake her. She was dying. He knew it. He couldn't lose her. There was only one option open to him. Reaching down, he grabbed her wrist and bit into the soft flesh. Choosing someone was meant to be done with the person's consent, but Billie was unconscious. He couldn't ask her. And he couldn't wait to see if she woke up.

She might never wake up.

Gulping down her blood, he counted the faint heartbeats, hoping he was fast enough. There. Slashing his own wrist open with his teeth, he held his arm over her mouth, blood dripping down onto her tongue. Nothing. She wasn't swallowing. Massaging her throat, he kept his wrist over her mouth. *Please, please, please respond.* And then he felt her throat move. One mouthful. Then two.

Drink more, he thought. *Drink everything.*

She had to survive.

"What the fuck?"

Vere's head whipped toward the stairwell, which was hidden in shadows. He didn't dare move the hand that was still over Billie's mouth. Vere saw that the speaker was the city guard from the reception area, dressed in his uniform, steel baton out and at the ready. The man was staring at him like he'd grown two heads, but Vere had the feeling the human had already assessed the entire room and knew exactly what was going on.

"Get out of here," Vere growled.

But the human had a death wish. He stepped closer. "What are you doing to her?"

"Trying to save her life."

"In case you hadn't heard, Choosing someone is illegal right now."

"If I don't, she'll die." Billie stopped drinking. He pulled his wrist back, hoping she'd taken enough. Vere rubbed the slice on his arm, which was already healing. "She still might die."

He had to keep her alive for another six days.

The human squatted down next to him. He ran a hand over his mouth, suddenly serious. "Shit. What the fuck did they do to her?"

"What does it look like?" Fatigue washed over him.

"You got them all?"

"Yes." He thought so, anyway.

"You need to move her."

"I can't. I think she has internal injuries."

"I'll be the judge of whether she can be moved." A small human woman entered the room, carrying a black leather bag that clinked when she moved. She had curly auburn hair, and the stench of formaldehyde cloaked the air around her.

"Alice?" The guard stood. "I told you to wait until I secured the scene."

"I couldn't hear the sounds of fighting, and I needed to check that Billie was okay. Move."

"Alice–"

"Kyle, *move*."

Alice knelt down next to Vere and opened her bag. "My name is Alice Reive, I am the City Coroner. You think she has internal trauma?"

Vere pointed to Billie's bruised stomach. "But don't coroner's work with dead bodies?"

"I'm a trained doctor." Then Alice swore.

"Kyle, get these bodies removed and then clean up after them."

"Me? Clean up?"

Alice was looking at Vere's wrist and Billie's mouth. "You started the process?"

She was a quick study, Vere had to give her that.

"Yes."

"It's illegal right now."

"I wasn't about to let her die."

Alice nodded at him. "Good man." She turned back to Kyle. "Only you and I can know about this.

Go upstairs and stop anyone else from coming down. Say it's a confidentiality matter or whatever you have to stop anyone from interfering. We can't move Billie right now, and probably not until the third or fourth day. Is that right?"

Vere nodded. "Takes three days to do the full blood transfer."

"The captain will want to know," Kyle said.

"If he asks, tell him. But we don't want Billie having to lie in this basement surrounded by rotting corpses in the meantime."

Alice was a cheery woman, Vere thought.

"What about the girl?" Kyle nodded at the human in the corner, who was staring at them with a dreamy look on her face. She hadn't screamed at all when he'd killed the two vampires in front of her.

"High." Alice stared at her for a few seconds. "We'll move her out of here. We need to get her to a medical facility anyway. She'll have broken bones and will need to go through detox. If she can go through detox."

Alice pulled out a stethoscope from her black bag. "Now, let's see if we can keep Billie alive for the next six days."

CHAPTER TWENTY-ONE

Billie didn't think that death was meant to hurt. At least, she was pretty sure she had been in pain. A lot of it. She remembered screaming in agony. Now she felt weightless. Almost like she was floating.

"Billie?"

Was someone with her?

Had someone else died, too?

"Billie? Come on, wake up."

Wake up? You couldn't just wake up from being dead. You were *dead*.

Or was she?

She'd survived being attacked once, maybe she'd managed to beat the odds a second time. But she'd been hurt badly this time. When she'd caressed Vere's cheek, she'd known the pain would finish what his brother had started.

"Billie! Wake up this instant!"

That was it. She wasn't about to be bossed around, even in death. "Don't tell me what to do!"

She opened her eyes.

Vere's face hovered over her, and she blinked. His brown hair was lit from behind, casting him in a soft glow. He looked even more handsome than she remembered. Although he smelled a bit cold – like iced coffee. "I'm alive?"

His face vanished and then Alice was there, her hair tied back in a messy bun, some medical contraption looped around her neck. Two fingers pressed to Billie's neck. "Pulse is good."

"Alice, move!"

"I'm checking her out!"

"She's awake, which means she made it. Can I have some time with her? *Please*."

Alice huffed. "Fine, you know where I'll be."

Vere's face returned to her field of vision. "Bye, Alice!" Billie said softly. Was any of this real?

"See you soon."

Then it was just her and Vere. She still couldn't really believe she was alive. But she'd survived once before...

Gently, he scooped a hand under her back and helped her sit up. "You made it."

"I'm dreaming." Billie shook her head.

Looking around the room, Billie didn't recognize her surroundings. She was on a wide bed, with a canopy framed in gray silk. Walls were decorated with expensive white and silver wallpaper, and a thick carpet covered the floor. Pretty furniture dotted the room. She felt out of place, disconnected.

"Where am I?"

Vere sat back on the edge of the bed. "In my room."

"Your room? At your brother's house?" She couldn't stop the way her voice pitched upward.

"No, in my new apartments." Vere ran a hand over his hair. "I hired them when I was sure you were going to survive."

"Oh. Thank you for keeping me alive."

He grimaced. "You're welcome. And I'm sorry–"

Then her memory kicked in. "Sorry you didn't tell me you were a *vampire*?"

"I'm sorry for that. I truly am." His expression was so earnest, her heart hurt. "But there's more."

Billie shifted so she could sit upright. The aching pain that had plagued her every waking moment was gone. In fact, *nothing* hurt. How long had she been out? "What do you mean, 'more'?" Billie leaned forward, and then sat back. Her hip hadn't even twinged when she'd done that.

She needed to get more of these pain killers.

"There was no way we could get you to a hospital in time to save you. So I had to do something without your permission." Vere was looking down at the white coverlet. His fingers tapped a little rhythm on the material.

"What something?"

But she had a feeling she knew. Her hip didn't hurt. And it had given her pain almost every waking moment she had after she'd come to in that hospital bed. And she was alive. She shouldn't have been able to survive the injuries her brother had inflicted.

He still wasn't looking at her. "I Chose you."

"You Chose me." She waited a few breaths, and then, "You fucking *Chose* me?"

Vere looked at her then, his gaze sharp. "You were going to die."

Billie was shouting. "Did you ever think I might not want to survive if I became a vampire?"

"I couldn't let you die."

"Maybe you should have."

"Billie–"

She thrust a hand out, warding him away. A strange kind of calm descended on her. "I was nearly killed – twice – by vampires. And then you Chose me without asking. That is *illegal*."

"You didn't deserve to die, and screw the law."

Fatigue washed over her. It was done. She couldn't change it. Not without dying. And she didn't want to give up. But she remembered the whole reason she'd met Vere in the first place. "Vampires only Choose their lovers or friends. And with the king's ban–"

"We were lovers."

"One time doesn't make us lovers."

"It would have been more than that if my asshole brother hadn't been such a fucking psychopath."

Billie winced at the rage she heard in his voice. So she hadn't just been a fling. "You lied to me about being a vampire. What else haven't you told me?"

"I'm a spy." His stare dropped back to the sheets.

"You're a *what*?" Well, she wouldn't have picked that. But then, she'd never seen him outside of his wanting to help her solve the case. And really, why would a normal aristo have wanted to help her with that?

Things suddenly started to make a lot more sense.

"A spy. It's why I travel a lot."

"Right. Anything else?"

"I love you."

Billie shook her head. "Sorry?"

Vere chuckled, a little mirthlessly. "I knew I was infatuated with you, with your strength and beauty. But when you almost died – I broke the law to Choose you, and I'd do it again. We could both be sentenced to death for it, and I haven't told King Johan yet. I wanted to make sure you survived first."

"You barely know me."

Vere scooted forward then, meeting her bewildered stare. He took her hands in his. "I may not know your favorite color, but I know that you meet every day with open arms. That you fight for what you believe in, no matter what. That you're strong minded. That you have a sense of humor. That you have friends who care about you and who you care about. And that you will defy any odds to win."

Wow.

"Vere, I–"

He pressed a gentle finger to her lips. It felt strange. And she realized it was because her *fangs* were dropping down. She began to pant.

Maybe I've got fangs.

Fangs.

Shutting her eyes, she wished she could go back. Tell Mikael that she couldn't deliver that bloody letter. But then, she wouldn't have met Vere. And for some reason, despite the lies and machinations, she didn't regret that.

But she was *furious*.

"You don't have to say anything back. But I made

my decision about you when I Chose you. You can take your time to make your decision about me."

Chapter Twenty-Two

"I don't typically make house visits, Vere."

Vere pretended calm. This was the king, and he was standing in Vere's new living room, dressed in a burgundy silk suit. And there were three palace guards waiting downstairs, ready and willing to burst into his apartment at the slightest sign of trouble.

"This is a special case," Vere said, voice level.

"So you keep saying." King Johan folded his arms across his chest.

Vere indicated the king should sit on one of the wingback chairs. Vere took the sofa after the monarch sat. "Well, it's to do with the City Guard kidnapping case."

"You could have told me about this at the palace."

"Not really."

"And why is that?"

"Because of me," Billie said. She bobbed an awkward bow. "Your Majesty."

She was standing in the doorway of the room,

dressed in loose blue pants and one of his white shirts. He'd asked her to dress a bit more formally, but she'd just smiled and shaken her head. She'd only been Chosen for a week, after all. And she wasn't feeling the best, despite her largely healed body.

King Johan stared at Billie for a few moments, then stood. Vere followed suit, but stayed put. The king strode over to her and then gently tilted her chin into the light, seeing her red-purple eyes. "Chosen." He inhaled. "Newly Chosen."

Vere watched as Billie stood there, appearing relaxed. But he bet she was worried. They'd talked about how they would break the news. They'd decided that privately was the best way. Vere didn't want to give the king a reason to enforce his new law in public.

Johan turned back to him, his eyes burning. "You've put me in a terrible position."

"Your Majesty, before you get too angry, I just want to say that Vere saved my life." The king's attention swung back to her. "I was the city guard who was abducted and then almost killed by an aristo vampire six months ago. I was also the guard who looked into the past case files and determined that this aristo had been kidnapping free humans for over a hundred years. And then, I was abducted again."

Billie swallowed and then raised a hand to her neck. The scar had almost faded completely when she was Chosen, but it hadn't quite disappeared. Just the faintest line remained. Vere thought it hadn't healed completely because her body had had to do so much to repair the other damage done to her.

"Not only did they slit my throat once, and dump me in the Thyme, but they came back for me. By the time Vere arrived, I was beaten to a bloody pulp and had no chance of surviving without his help. It was only because we were lovers – and that he knew who the attacker was – that he managed to save me."

King Johan turned back to him. "You knew who it was? Why didn't you tell me?"

"I worked it out the morning she was kidnapped again. It was my brother."

Johan frowned, and then went back to his seat. He indicated the two of them should also sit. "Word is that Bryce is on a holiday."

The king always was across the gossip that floated through the streets of Pinton. How he managed to stay so up to date and run the country was a feat that impressed Vere.

"He's dead," Vere's voice was flat. "But to save a scandal, I let it slip he was on a holiday. He will tragically 'die' when away, and we shall publicly mourn his terrible loss."

The monarch was silent for some time. Then he nodded. "We shall say that the two of you were lovers, and that you had just been diagnosed with a fatal illness. Human medicine could not save you, and so you had to be Chosen. I gave my consent, despite the ban, because you would not survive until I lifted it. Your kidnapping case will go unsolved. Is that clear?"

Billie nodded.

"What about the body?"

"Already cremated. The coroner kept it quiet."

They owed Alice a few favors after all this.

The king stood and looked at Billie. "I am going to have enough of a debacle with you being Chosen, let alone if word gets out that Vere's brother was killing humans he'd plucked off the street. I need the humans in this city to feel safe."

Not be *safe.*

Feel safe.

Interesting choice of words. Vere didn't know what Billie was thinking, but he was grateful that they weren't going to be executed for treason.

The king turned to leave, but he was shaking his head. "Make sure when you formerly present her to court, she is properly dressed. Now I am going to have two City Guard vampires. Who would have thought?"

Vere saw King Johan out, and returned to Billie. He couldn't stop smiling, nor did he want to. "We aren't going to be executed."

Billie grinned, but then her look soured.

"What is it?"

"This bloody nausea. It won't go away."

Vere frowned. She'd been feeling sick since her first sip of blood. "Maybe you need some human food with your blood. Your transformation was more traumatic than normal."

"Ergh. Food."

He grabbed her hand, but she pulled away from him. He frowned. "Come on, let's find you something to eat."

"Vere, wait a second."

He stopped.

Billie looked at him, her long dark hair loose around her face. She was so beautiful it made his teeth ache. "I just wanted to thank you for giving me this second chance at life. Even if I am plagued with nausea. But I can't go and pretend everything is okay. You lied to me."

He wasn't going to argue that he hadn't lied; he'd just kept quiet about his race. He'd known she probably would have run in the other direction had she been aware, and he'd chased her anyway. He'd been in the wrong. "I'm sorry."

She headed for the small kitchen. "I know. But I need time."

Well, they both certainly had nothing but time now.

CHAPTER TWENTY-THREE

Alice took a seat opposite Billie in Vere's drawing room. "How are things going?" She was wearing her red and black work clothes, and she smelt of formaldehyde. She must have come here straight from work.

Billie rang for tea and biscuits. While her new life had taken some adjustment, she hadn't minded gaining servants, even if she felt bad about asking them to help her. She'd been living with Vere for a month now, and things were…awkward. He'd been caring, solicitous, and kind, but she'd been distant and angry. His understanding only served to annoy her more.

"Not well," Billie admitted. Alice had visited her a few times since Billie had been Chosen, but the coroner was busy. And Billie had been pretending everything was better than it was.

"I thought so," Alice said.

Billie clenched her fists in her lap. "How come?"

"You look frustrated. At first, I thought it was

because of my blood – me smelling like dinner for you. But then I saw you with Vere, and I gathered things weren't going well." Alice shrugged.

"He *lied* to me." And Alice smelled less like food than other humans, mostly because of the formaldehyde stench. But she wasn't about to tell the coroner that.

"How so?"

"He didn't tell me he was a vampire. That his brother was some kind of crazed killer."

Alice met her gaze, her brown eyes serious. "But you never asked. He never told you he was human, you just assumed."

"But–"

"And you're right. He knew his brother was crazy, but he didn't know he was a killer, not like that. He told me as much when I had the body cremated. He'd already spoken to the king about his brother's behavior with his slaves years ago and got his family banned from owning them. He'd tried to fix the problem."

Billie gritted her teeth. He'd told her that, too. "But Bryce still went around killing!"

Alice's voice was calm. "And that isn't Vere's fault. Just because someone's related to a killer, doesn't make them a bad person, too."

No, Billie knew that. Drat it.

"But–"

Alice came to sit next to Billie. She gently took one of Billie's hands in her own. "Be angry at the people who deserve it."

Billie's shoulders slumped. "I just–"

Alice waited.

"I'm just so mad at myself for wanting to believe he was human, that I blinded myself to his race."

"And yet, the fact he was a vampire meant he could save your life."

Billie bit her lip.

The servant came in then, and deposited a tray of biscuits and tea on the delicate coffee table. They thanked him and he left with a smile. Alice leaned forward, inhaling the rich aroma of the tea. "Come now, let's eat."

"You eat, I still feel a little nauseous."

Alice frowned. "Still?"

"It comes and goes."

"Hrm."

Billie didn't like the sound of that.

Alice picked up a piece of shortbread. "Now, enough of that. Let me fill you in on what's been happening at work..."

Chapter Twenty-Four

Billie paced the length of her bedchamber. She'd left a note in Vere's room, asking him to meet her here whenever he got home. But she'd been too nervous to rest while she waited for him. Plus, her conversation with Alice was weighing on her mind. Billie had been so angry with Bryce – and with herself – that she'd been blaming Vere the whole time.

He could have walked out on her, but he hadn't. He'd stayed in the apartment – ostensibly to keep up appearances for the king – but she knew he could have left had he wanted to. And she'd repaid him by being cranky, angry and cold.

Sure, he hadn't told her he was a vampire, but she had a feeling that if she'd asked, he would have done.

A knock sounded on the door, and then Vere was standing in the doorway. "Billie?"

Billie came to a stop. "Come in."

Vere stepped into the room, shutting the door behind him. He was in a shirt, breeches and socks, his hair loose around his shoulders. "Are you okay? I got your note."

She gulped. He really was horribly handsome.

"Not really."

He stepped closer.

"I wanted to apologize," she began.

"Apologize?"

"I've been hard to live with. I know. But it's been difficult for me. I don't trust easily, and I'd trusted you. When I found out you were a vampire, and your brother–" she took a deep breath "–and your brother was the man who nearly killed me, it hurt."

"Billie–"

"It hurt because I thought I'd been a fool. That I'd been so desperate to think that someone could like me, broken as I was, that I overlooked your base nature."

Vere winced.

"But I was wrong. Yes, you hadn't told me you were a vampire, but you're a kind person. Caring. Nothing like your brother, and I'm sorry I tarred you with the same brush."

There. She'd said it. Most of it.

Vere came closer. "Billie, you don't have to apologize to me for *anything*."

"I–"

"I love you, Billie. And I just want you to be happy. If being mad at me helps you, then be mad."

He loved her. He'd said it before, but she hadn't really believed him. But actions spoke louder than words. And he'd proven that he cared for her.

She closed the distance between them, throwing her arms around him. He hugged her back, tightly.

Billie felt safe. Finally, she felt safe. "I love you, too." A sob caught in her throat, and then another.

♦

Later, he still held her, arms gentle, hands smoothing over her hair. "Feel better?"

Billie nodded, her cheek rubbing against his shirt, which was damp from her crying. She felt like her tears had washed her clean. "I want to go back to work."

"What?"

"I need something to do. I am going crazy staying here. I need a purpose, something to think about, other than myself and what happened."

"Billie, you're still not one hundred percent recovered from being Chosen."

"I have a desk job."

"You're a vampire. They don't work for the guard."

"Elle Brown's a vampire and she does."

"You aren't Elle. And you don't have to work."

"But I want to."

"Give it a few months."

"A week."

"A month."

"Two weeks."

She leaned back, and gave him a watery smile. "Done."

EPILOGUE

Three months later

"You puked all over that guy!" Kyle was still laughing.

Billie wanted to smack him over the head, but she was a vampire now, and that could give him a concussion. "I didn't mean to."

They were in the morgue, which was located under the City Guard offices, waiting for Alice. They were in the first half of the large room, and a single shrouded cadaver was in the corner of the second. A stone bench ran along the wall behind them, and its surface was so shiny, she could see her reflection in it.

"Man, the look on his face!"

Billie gave a small laugh then. It had been pretty funny, after she'd wiped the vomit from her mouth, and gotten over the utter mortification of losing her lunch on someone's chest. She'd gone out with Kyle to attend a domestic dispute, as Elle – his normal partner – was off duty. They'd had to smash their way into a small apartment, where they'd found a human man trying to beat his wife to death. She and Kyle had leapt in to pull him off the poor woman, and then she'd done it. Vomited. All over the guy.

Then the wife-beating husband had lost his last meal. All over himself.

"The look on whose face?" Vere's voice entered the room and the conversation.

Billie turned narrowed eyes on Kyle. The guard held up his hands. "Hey, he wanted to know if you were still sick, and so I sent a little note around. Not my fault he's overprotective and rushed over here to see if you were okay."

"Right."

"I'll go on my way now." Kyle high-tailed it out the room, just as Alice entered.

"Hi, Billie."

"Hey, Alice."

"Still feeling sick?"

Billie nodded. So everyone was on to her. But Billie had asked Alice to come and meet her here. There were very few doctors in Pinton who knew as much about vampire anatomy as Alice did. And Billie didn't know any of them.

"I am going to give you an examination, so can your lovely partner wait upstairs?"

Vere's eyebrows rose. "Me? Wait upstairs?"

"Go away and let me spend some time with the doctor."

Vere mumbled something under his breath and left.

Alice pulled on some gloves. "Now, let's get to

work."

Billie didn't have a great feeling about this.

◆

"I'm *what*?" Billie sat down on the morgue's only chair with a *thunk*.

Vere was back downstairs, and from the way he was swaying on his feet, she wondered if he was about to topple over. Could she reach him in time if he fell? "That's impossible."

Alice put her clipboard down on the stone bench with a click. "Almost impossible."

Vere was shaking his head, which probably wasn't helping with his overall stability. "But, *how*?"

Alice shrugged. "The usual way, I suspect."

Vere frowned. "Are you sure?"

"I know how to diagnose a pregnancy, thank you very much." Alice put one of her hands on her hip.

"But, Chosen vampires are infertile." Vere had waited to tell Billie that until after she'd forgiven him. He'd been careful, and quiet, and worried that she wouldn't take the news well. But she was alive. And happy. She'd just been grateful for that. Children hadn't ever really been factored into her lifestyle.

"Yes. Normally. However, I think you might have conceived during the blood transfer."

"When I was dying." Billie couldn't keep the disbelief out of her voice.

"But we had sex the night before, not that day. And definitely not *during*."

"Sperm can survive for three to five days in the

body. Not so long outside of it. Billie must have ovulated just before you Chose her. The pregnancy probably wouldn't have taken, if you hadn't provided vampire blood to help sustain it. But you did. I always wondered why all of Billie's scars never healed up completely, but this makes sense. Her body was giving those resources to sustain the pregnancy."

"I thought it was because of the severity of the injury," Vere said.

Alice shrugged. "Maybe. But the evidence seems to point to my theory. Plus, vampire sperm is pretty hardy. It possibly could have survived even a week within Billie."

Billie raised an eyebrow, impressed, and a little disturbed by her friend's knowledge. "How come you know so much about vampire sperm?"

Alice gave a quick, strange smile. "I'm writing a paper on it. Anyway, congratulations. I'll give you guys some privacy."

"I can't believe it." Billie said after Alice was gone.

"Neither can I."

Looking up, Billie met Vere's stunned gaze. She'd never seen him floored before. It was kind of funny. But not really, given the circumstances. "Do you want the baby?"

"Do you?"

She hadn't ever thought about children. But this one was a miracle. And it was theirs. "I do."

Vere leaned forward, wrapping his arms around her. "I didn't think we could have children, but now, the idea of a little girl running around looking like you, I can't wait for it."

"It could be a boy."

"It's a girl," Vere said.

"You don't know that."

They stayed together for a long time, the smell of preserving fluids, decay and stone permeating the air. Then Billie thought of something she hadn't considered. "What if there's something wrong, because I was partly human at the time?"

Vere kissed the top of her head. "Then we'll deal with it. But I wouldn't worry. The baby will be perfect."

She looked up at him. "How can you be so sure?"

"Because you're her mother. And you can do anything."

ACKNOWLEDGMENTS

Publishing is never a certain road, and I want to thank those of you have stood by me through the journey so far: my husband, my family, my writing friends, my agent, and you, the readers. Specifically, I want to thank my wonderful beta reader Joanne Danton and my editor supreme, Pete Kempshall. *Survivor* is a small story, but one that continues to share glimpses of the strange, terrible, and sometimes wonderful world of the Graced. I hope you enjoyed it!

Amanda Pillar is an award-winning editor and author who lives in Victoria, Australia, with her husband and two cats.

Amanda is the author of the Graced series, and has had numerous short stories published. She has co-edited six fiction anthologies and solo-edited two: *Bloodstones* and *Bloodlines*, published by Ticonderoga Publications.

In her day job, she works as an archaeologist.